FALLING FOR A HOOD KING 3

SHVONNE LATRICE

ABOUT THE AUTHOR

<u>Other Works by Me:</u>

Good Girls Love Thugs 1-5
Falling for a Hood King 1-4
Married to a Distinguished Thug 1-3
She's Gotta Have It 1-2
Me & My Dope Boy 1-3
Yazir & Nina 1-3
Forbidden Love with a Thug 1-3
You Needed Me 1-3
Shorty is in Love with a Real One 1-4
I Got Your Back 1-2
My Baby Is a West Coast King 1-4
Our Love Is the Realest 1-3
She Got It Bad for a Heartless Gangsta 1-4
She Got It Bad for a Heartless Gangsta: An AK Christmas
Hood Boyz Fall In Love Too 1-3
Nobody Can Love You Like Them Roughnecks Do 1-4
She Gave Her All to the Hood's Finest 1-5

Visit www.theshvonnelatrice.com for paperbacks!

facebook.com/ShvonneLatrice

twitter.com/shvonnelatrice

instagram.com/shvonnelatrice

$14.99
ISBN 978-1-966375-01-2

"You have to push now Mrs. Tate!" the doctor yelled to me, as I rocked slowly in pain. I was at the hospital about to deliver my daughter, but I needed my husband here with me.

"I can't! I have to wait until the father gets here," I replied, plopping my head down on the pillow.

The pain was unbearable. Just like with Jackson, the time to push came before the damn epidural could kick in, so this was a natural birth. There wasn't a pain worse than pushing a human out of my body without any medicine.

The doctor stood up and paced the delivery room defeated. He and the nurse had been begging me to push for the last five minutes. No matter what they said, I refused until Julius arrived. He couldn't miss this. Suddenly, Rashad was let in and he had a worried look on his face. Rashad wore his thoughts on his face and when there was a problem, he showed it. I was in too much pain right now; I couldn't take anymore. *God, please let Julius be alive*, I prayed silently.

"Rashad, where is Julius?" I asked sweating profusely. I was still rocking slowly to help ease the pain that I was experiencing.

"He got arrested ma," Rashad shook his head.

"What?" I yelled making the pain temporarily leave my body.

"Mrs. Tate, your baby needs to come out," the doctor let me know. Didn't he just hear that my husband was in jail? He was pissing me off at this point.

"Natalia, you need to push ma. Julius ain't gone make it," Rashad added. His eyes pleaded with me, but I just didn't want to do it. This was supposed to be perfect and right now it was far from it.

I didn't say anything in response, as I turned away from Rashad. I hated Julius right now, even though it wasn't his fault he wasn't here. Then again, it was his fault. Why was he always doing things that sent him to jail? He knew I would be giving birth any minute, yet he went out and did something stupid to get thrown in jail. I hated him as much as I loved him right now.

"Mrs. Tate," the doctor said, snapping me back from my thoughts.

"If you let Benjamin come talk to me after this, then I will push." I looked up at Rashad and he nodded to say okay.

I grabbed onto the sides of the hospital bed since I didn't have my husband's hand to hold, and began to push my baby out. I thought I would pass out, because it felt like my body was ripping open. Winnie was filming because Julius wasn't here to do it his damn self. I plopped down on the bed as soon as I heard my daughter's first cry. Seeing my new baby gave me some happiness in this horrible situation.

Our daughter, Harmony Giselle Tate was finally here, and she was so beautiful. From what I could tell already, she looked just like her jailbird father. I kissed her cheek, and then handed her back to the nurse to lay her down in the plastic crib. All I could think about was Rashad's promise to me. I was about to call him on the phone, until the hospital door opened.

"Good morning Mrs. Tate," Julius' lawyer, Benjamin walked in.

"You can call me Natalia," I smiled and he nodded.

Benjamin was an older black man with a salt and pepper beard. He always smelled good and only wore neutral colored tan suits. He was really nice and always made me think about what it would've been like to have an actual father. I wondered if he had kids.

"Okay, so it looks like they have arrested Julius for child abduction."

"What? He kidnapped a child?" I asked trying to sit up.

What the hell was going on? Shit like this made me want to involve myself more in what Julius did on the daily. He always wanted me to keep my nose out of his business for my safety, but at this point, I was thinking that it wasn't such a good idea for me not to get involved.

"Well, we know he wouldn't do that. After speaking with him over the phone, it appears Bianca kidnapped a young woman's child and she sent the authorities after her. Julius was just in the wrong place at the wrong time." Benjamin shook his head.

"So, then why is he still there?" I frowned in confusion. This really wasn't making any sense to me. One thing that *was* making sense though, was that Bianca had lost her finger-licking mind.

"Well, he has to go to trial. It seems the child's mother believes that Julius and Bianca were in on this together. She explained that Bianca told her on multiple occasions that she and Julius were working together in whatever scheme she had going on. Bianca was using this girl in order to support her lie to Julius that she was pregnant. But don't worry, we have plenty witnesses willing to testify on Julius' behalf, proving that Bianca was obsessed with him. On top of that, the young lady has already admitted to the detectives that Bianca's pregnancy was a fake," he replied.

"When is the trial?" I asked while still trying to process that people like Bianca weren't just in Lifetime movies.

"In a month," he nodded.

I was furious right now. I hated this Bianca bitch more than I had ever hated her before. I knew something was strange about her pregnancy, and low and behold, she was faking it. I felt so bad for turning my back on Julius when he needed me the most. I should've stuck by him like I promised him I would. I wasn't acting like a wife at all, but that was going to change.

"So when can I see him?" I asked.

"You can visit him when you get out of here," Benjamin smiled sympathetically.

I liked him and I was happy that we had him to defend Julius. Benjamin had been a high-powered lawyer all his life, until he found out he had cancer. He became so sick that he lost his practice and had no clients. By the grace of God, he was cured, but he was having a hard time building his clientele and practice back up. Being the generous, loving, guy that he is, Julius hired him on because he knew how good he was. Despite what everyone may think of Julius, he was a great man. As long as his kids and I knew that, no one else's opinion mattered.

I finally smiled back and then laid back down on the bed. I was still in pain from giving birth. I had some tearing just like last time, so I had to be stitched up which was not pleasant. As Benjamin was getting up, there was a knock on the hospital door.

"Come in," I called out wondering who it was. I wished it was Julius, but I knew that wasn't the case.

"Hey baby," Marlon walked in smiling.

Benjamin looked confused as to why this strange man was addressing me in such a way. I had totally forgotten that I'd just gotten into a relationship with him. I was regretting that decision more and more as each second passed. All I wanted right now was to be with Julius, and Marlon was a far cry from him.

"I will call you later," I said to Benjamin as he headed out and he nodded. I prayed to God he didn't mention this little encounter to Julius. Knowing him, he would start saying the baby wasn't his. "What are you doing here, Marlon?" I finally asked. I tried to mask my tone of disappointment.

"Well, my baby just had a baby," he smiled and handed me some flowers. I cringed at the sound of him calling me baby again. Marlon was a cool guy and maybe before Julius, he may have had a chance, but that wasn't the case and I wasn't feeling him.

"It's not your baby though, you didn't have to-" I was cut off by a kiss on the lips.

I pulled away because it didn't feel right. I didn't get hot all over and my body didn't tingle like it did when I kissed Julius. All I could think about was how I was going to get rid of this man without hurting his feelings.

"So what did you name the girl?" he asked as he sat down in the chair smiling.

***

I was finally home from the hospital and I wasted no time getting ready to go see Julius. I couldn't wait to see his sexy face and let him know how sorry I was for running out on him.

I was already dressed and so were Harmony and Jackson. I'd finally buckled them in my car, when my phone rang. I rolled my eyes when I saw Marlon's name on my screen.

"Hey," I said dryly.

"Good morning babe. What are you doing?" he asked.

For some reason Marlon seemed like he was my age, even though he was twenty-one like Julius. Julius seemed so much more mature. Marlon was so sensitive and always really giddy, like a little boy. It was such a turn off that even his good looks couldn't make up for. *Just dump him Natalia; you know you don't want this*, I thought.

"I'm about to go visit Julius," I replied cranking my BMW.

"Oh, I feel you. For how long?" he asked sounding sad.

"A couple of hours. Not too long," I responded trying to ease his mind. *Why did I care?* I thought.

"Aight, hit me up when you get back," he said.

"Mm hmm," I mumbled before quickly disconnecting.

JULIUS TATE

I could kill Bianca's psycho ass right now. She really took it to the extreme, and for what? How long did she think she could keep this whole baby thing up? The bitch kidnapped someone's baby! That hoe is a straight up looney toon for fucking real. I really don't know what happened to her, because the Bianca I knew would never do no shit like that. One of the reasons I even agreed to make her my girl in the past, was because I knew she would never key my car, set me up, or do anything that would harm me. I guess that's what good dick will do to these hoes; turn a sane chick into a psychopath. Regardless of what part I had in it, as soon as I got out she was getting murked.

"Tate, visitor!" the C.O. yelled as he pulled the cell gate open.

I hopped my ass up quick because I already knew who it was. Rashad had already been to see me, so I knew it was my baby girl. I couldn't wait to see her pretty face, although I hadn't been away from her for long. I missed my son too, so I had hoped that she brought him with her. I couldn't wait to explain all this bullshit to her, so that we could get back together. I needed her to know that Bianca had played the both of us.

I finally made it to the visitation room and was stunned to see her with two babies. *Why didn't Rashad tell me she gave birth?* I asked myself. Maybe he didn't want me stressing. When I neared her, a smile spread across her beautiful face. She stood up and I hugged her tight with Jackson in the middle. I kissed her lips and then his cheek. My eyes darted back to the beautiful baby girl in the carrier and I couldn't believe she was here already. I looked over at the guard and he nodded to say it was okay for me to hold her. Natalia sat Jackson on the visiting table and then pulled our daughter out for me to hold.

"You named her Harmony like we decided?" I asked looking down at her. She smelled so good and she was a perfect mix of Natalia and me. I laughed because Jackson looked identical to *me only*.

"Of course," she smiled and I kissed her lips again.

This shit was crazy to me right now; the fact that I was a married man with kids. The old Julius is probably looking at me with his jaw on the ground. I wouldn't change this shit for the world though. I just hated that instead of being a husband and father, I was sitting behind bars like a fuck up.

I handed Harmony back to Natalia, after kissing her little cheeks. I eyed Natalia's body as she put my daughter back into the carrier and sat down.

"Your body looks good already," I said almost as if I thought it was magic.

She still had a stomach, but it was quickly going down. It always amazed me how quick her body reverted. I always thought you kept the baby weight on for a couple months, but not Natalia. After a couple weeks, she was back to her small self.

"Thank you," she blushed. "I'm sorry about leaving you; I should've stuck by you like I promised I would have. I love you Julius and I won't ever do anything like that again," she added.

"Nah, you're good ma. You didn't know. Shit, I didn't know she wasn't really pregnant," I shrugged. "And I love you too, Mrs. Tate," I smiled and she blushed harder.

"Benjamin said it looks good for you though," she smiled.

"Yeah I know, but I'm gone be in here for a damn month," I said exhaling heavily and looking at my son sitting in Natalia's lap. What kind of example was I setting for him? I needed to get my shit together.

"Well, we will be here when you get out," she said rubbing my hand.

"You better be girl." I bit my lip as I stared at her lustfully.

She hadn't given me any pussy in a while. When I get out of here, I may get her pregnant again. "I'm sorry I missed the birth," I added. It was bothering me more than she thought. That's one thing I never wanted to miss, when I had kids.

"It's okay, Winnie recorded the video for you this time," she chuckled. "And cut the cord," she continued and we both laughed.

We continued to have good conversation until Harmony started to cry. I really didn't want my family to leave, but I knew it was a consequence of me being in jail. With every bad thing I experienced by being locked up, I told myself Bianca was going to pay for it with her life.

ONE WEEK LATER

I didn't feel comfortable having Marlon over the house, so we always went to his place or to the old condo Julius and I used to have. I was scared as hell that someone would tell Julius I was still dating Marlon, but I just couldn't break it off with him. I wanted to, believe me, but it was easier said than done. I felt bad for him and a part of me wanted to keep him stashed away in case Julius did me dirty again. What if I let something good go, just to end up alone again? I wasn't doing that.

I appreciated Winnie so much, because she would come with me when I would entertain Marlon at the condo. I also appreciated the fact that I knew she wouldn't mention this to Julius. Winnie was like a best friend/mom to me, and I was so thankful for her. At the moment, she was upstairs in her old room watching TV, while Jackson and Harmony were asleep. I had my baby monitors next to me because I didn't want to bother Winnie anymore; she'd done enough.

"So, I was thinking we could go to breakfast tomorrow," Marlon offered as we watched Martin reruns. Winnie had just made dinner so we were good and full.

"I can't tomorrow. We can go Friday," I smiled as I sipped some sparkling water.

"Well, what are you doing tomorrow that's stopping you from going?" he frowned and sipped his champagne.

"I-I'm going to see Julius," I said and waited with bated breath for his response. *You should've told him something else Natalia,* I thought.

"Here we fucking go. You acting like he yo' nigga Nat," he said slamming his champagne flute on the coffee table. I wanted to tell him that he was right but decided against it.

"No I'm not," was all I could say.

"Yes you are. You're still rocking your wedding ring and that fucking gold chain around your neck. Let a nigga know what's up, because I can be on my way," he shook his head.

I should've taken him up on his offer, but I was being selfish. I wish I could tell him to just wait on the sidelines in case Julius messed up, but I knew that he wouldn't.

"No, Marlon. I just… this stuff means nothing. I'm just used to wearing it," I lied. I felt bad saying my wedding ring and promise chain meant nothing after all that stuff I was just telling Julius.

Why didn't I just let him go? I didn't want to be with him at all, no matter how hard I tried to make myself like him. I knew I only wanted Julius, so why not let Marlon be on his way? I don't know. Marlon was a regular guy. I knew he wasn't extremely sought after like Julius, and I knew he wouldn't do anything I didn't like. Although Julius had changed, he was still capable of doing me wrong. I was trying to be with Marlon for the wrong reasons, but oh well. Maybe I would learn to like him as more than a friend overtime.

"I'll take your word for it then," he smirked and scooted closer to me.

He wrapped his arm around my body and started to kiss my neck. I wanted him to stop but he was already suspicious of my feelings for Julius. He rubbed his hand up my thigh and I thought I was going to throw up.

"Marlon, I'm healing, remember," I said, happy I thought of a cop out.

"Damn, I forgot. How much longer?" he asked biting his lip.

"Four more weeks," I lied and moved his hand from under my

dress. It was only two more weeks, but he didn't need to know that. I gave myself an extra two weeks to hopefully give myself time to think of another lie.

"Shit, well in four weeks be ready," he chuckled and I fake laughed for his sake. "I think I'm in love with you Nat," he added as he stared into my eyes.

"Y-you a-are?" I stammered and swallowed the lump in my throat, as he pushed my hair behind my ear. How could he love me when I barely like him? This was all the way off.

"Yeah I am. What do you think about that?" he asked licking his lips.

"Uh, I appreciate it?" I shrugged and he laughed. I may lie to him about everything else, but I wasn't gonna say that I loved him.

He dipped his tongue into my mouth and pulled me in close. He was drooling all down my chin and was even wetting up the tip of my nose. I'd only kissed two guys in my life, not including him, and he was by far the worst I'd ever experienced. It seemed that the more time we spent together, the less I liked him. It was supposed to be the opposite.

"Okay, Marlon," I said lightly pushing him off.

"Just let me eat it," he said in a breathy tone.

"Marlon-" he cut me off by dipping his tongue back into my mouth. "Marlon, stop! I told you I need four more weeks," I frowned and pushed him off.

"Damn, chill Natalia!" he frowned.

"I'm gonna go to bed. I will see you tomorrow," I said standing up.

He stared up at me for a couple seconds and then scoffed. He shook his head and stood up to leave. I walked him to the door and opened it so he could hurry and get out. He pulled me close and kissed my lips again until I lightly pushed him off. Ugh!

"See you later babe. I love you," he winked and walked out.

I slammed the door without saying anything at all. I wasn't sure how long I could keep this up with him.

JULIUS

VERDICT DAY

Today was the day that I would possibly go home to my family and work. I was feeling good since Benjamin said I had nothing to worry about. I couldn't wait to walk out of that courtroom as a free man. From this day forward, I was gonna do everything in my power to not go back to jail.

I was led into the courtroom and I saw my beautiful wife, kids and Winnie. Natalia was wearing an all-black dress and she looked sexy as hell. I smirked at her as she held Harmony, and she smirked back. I couldn't wait to be tearing that shit up tonight. I just prayed that my confidence in the fact that I would leave a free man, wasn't in vain. I looked over some more and smiled when I saw Rashad, Tim, Dash and Leese. They were my niggas and they forever had my back.

The judge walked out and Benjamin gave me a pat on the back to let me know everything was okay. He knew I was nervous even though he assured me multiple times that I was going home today. I nodded and stood up along with everyone else in the courtroom. After the bailiff said his piece, everyone sat back down so the verdict could be read.

One of the jurors walked a piece of paper over to the judge so that he could read whether or not I was guilty. If I was guilty, I would spend three years in jail and that could not fucking happen. My son would be in pre-school and talking, and my daughter would be three years old and walking. There was no way I was missing that much of their lives. I tell you one thing though, if I did, Bianca would suffer.

I took a deep breath and kept replaying all the witnesses that spoke on how obsessed Bianca was with me, and how I had no idea she wasn't really pregnant. The Lizzie chick, the one whose baby was stolen, testified that she had never met or spoken to me, which helped.

"On the single count of child abduction charges, we the jury find the defendant Julius Christian Tate, not guilty," she read it and I let out a huge sigh of relief.

Benjamin hugged me tightly and my family members cheered and hugged one another. I turned around to wink at Natalia as a single tear slid down her face. I wanted to hurry up and get the hell out of there before something changed.

"You're dismissed Mr. Tate and for future references, please only stick to one woman at a time," the judge said and hit his gavel down.

I chuckled and nodded, before turning around to exit with everyone else. I'd been in jail twice in less than a year, and I prayed this was the last damn time. I was gone definitely take the judge's advice and stick to my one and only baby girl.

As soon as I reached her, I pulled her into my arms and tongued her down. I took Jackson from her, and let Winnie carry Harmony in the carrier. We headed out the courtroom, where my boys Tim, Dash, and Leese, dapped me up. My brother, Rashad pulled me into a hug and patted my back. I kissed Natalia's lips constantly, as we walked towards the car. I was happy as a dog in a hubcap factory right now.

"I've been missing you, daddy," Natalia said walking into our room from the bathroom.

I was lying on the bed in my boxers and the room was lit up with candles only. She smiled and strutted over to me in her lingerie set, looking just as sexy as she did before the baby. She had on a navy blue lace set that was see-through. Her small, perky breasts looked scrumptious and her caramel complexion was nothing less than perfection.

"Get over here," I said tucking my lips in. I'd been craving her pretty ass.

She giggled at my dick standing straight up through my boxers, and then straddled me. I pulled her close and unhooked her bra with the quickness. I cupped her breasts and just admired them for a while, before sucking her nipples. I was squeezing her little plump ass with all my might, as I devoured her hard nipples.

"Ahh," she moaned throwing her head back.

After getting my fix, I flipped her on all fours and tugged down her panties. I ran my tongue along the slit of her pussy and inhaled the sweet scent. I planted soft kisses on it that made her shiver a little bit. I slowly started to French kiss it, making her cry out. I spread her legs some more and started to suck her clit harder from the back.

"I'm cumming Ju," she whimpered.

She released into my mouth and I kept sucking and licking until she came again. I removed my boxers and then stood up on my knees. She turned around to take my dick into her warm, wet mouth. She teased the head for a bit, getting her mouth to become nice and drenched.

"Fuck," I moaned as she bobbed up and down on my rod. "Suck it just like that, Nat." I bit my lip and ran my fingers through her soft long hair.

"Mm," she cooed as she brought her hand up to play with my balls.

"I'm cumming, shit," I grunted.

She sped up some more and I busted down her throat. She swallowed it up and cleaned every drop off of the tip. My body jerked a bit and I think my toes curled. She slid her mouth off of my dick and smiled.

"Get your sexy ass on this dick," I demanded and laid down.

She climbed atop my rock hard member and started to sit on it. She was hesitant, because we hadn't had sex in a while and she just ended her healing period. I flipped her on her back and got between her sexy legs.

"You gotta take this dick baby girl," I whispered as I kissed her neck.

I positioned my head at her opening, and she tensed up a bit. I looked up and stared into her eyes, before kissing her passionately.

"You gotta relax and let me in, okay babe?" I said into her mouth as we kissed.

"Okay," she said in a low tone and finally relaxed her body.

I placed her legs over my forearms and stared into her eyes. I pushed into her tight, wet hole and almost nutted on contact. Got damn! I slowly pumped into her, until I was all the way in comfortably. She cried out in pain a little and tried to move up. I placed her up against the headboard so that she had nowhere to go, and then pushed the rest of my dick into her. I made sure to go extremely slow until she adjusted to my girth.

"I see you ain't been giving my pussy away," I said as I slowly stroked her.

"Never," she replied. "Ahhh, uhhh, slow Julius," she cried as I sucked her lips.

I pinned her hands behind her head and sucked on her neck, as I thrusted into her slowly like she wanted.

NATALIA

As soon as Julius left to go handle business, I hopped up and got ready to visit Marlon. He'd been blowing me up all night, to the point where I had to put my phone on Do Not Disturb *and* on silent. Once I did, I put it at the bottom of my purse for extra protection.

I'd lied to him the day before and told him I was just gonna hear the verdict and then come over to his apartment afterwards. We all know what happened instead though. It's not my fault. I missed my husband and after we all went out to dinner, Winnie included, one thing led to another. I didn't regret it though, because fucking Julius all night was what I wanted to do.

"Okay Winnie, I will be back in a couple hours. I'm uh, going to see Lucy," I smiled at her. I didn't want to make her lie for me anymore, so it was just best that she didn't even know.

"Okay Mrs. Tate. Don't worry, the babies will be fine," she smiled.

"I know," I smiled back and headed out. I had to walk slowly, because I was sore as hell from last night. A month in jail seemed to up Julius' sex drive. My vagina was so sore that I could barely wash it in the shower.

During the drive to Marlon's house, I was trying to think of something I could tell him. What reason could I give as to why I'd been gone all night and couldn't answer one of his fifteen calls and texts? I hated lying and it seemed like the more time I spent with Marlon, the more lies I had to tell.

I finally arrived to his apartment and took a deep breath. *Okay Natalia,* I told myself as I walked up his complex's stairs. I paused for a couple seconds and then lightly knocked on the door. I kind of hoped he wasn't home or that he didn't hear me knocking, so I could just *say* I stopped by.

"Fuck was you at all damn night?" he asked, swinging the door open with an angry expression.

He was wearing basketball shorts and had his shirt off. He had a nice little body but his arms weren't as strong looking as Julius'.

"I was with Lucy, she was having some problems," I replied nervously as I walked in past him.

"Is that right?" he asked folding his arms over his chest.

"That's what I said," I responded sitting down on his couch.

"I saw you leaving the courtroom with your husband. Y'all were kissing and shit, looking pretty fucking cozy to me," he squinted his eyes.

"I-I was just excited Marlon, I-"

"You looked in love to me Natalia. I'm gone ask you one more time, do you want to be with that nigga?" he said pointing his finger in my face.

"No!" I lied.

"Good," he replied plopping down next to me. "I ain't gone let you go anyway," he continued. *What?*

He grabbed my hand and kissed the back of it a couple times with his eyes closed. He then pulled me close to him and kissed on my neck as he ran his hands up to my jean zipper. I pushed him off as he tugged on my jeans.

"What now Natalia?" he frowned.

"I just need time Marlon. I'm still married and Julius really hurt me," I replied. I was really laying it on thick. Hopefully this would work, because there was no way I could have sex with him. "I don't want to have sex with anyone right now, it's not just you," I added. Plus, I was sore as fuck. It was no way I could spread my legs again for another dick down.

"Time for what? I have needs Natalia. You don't understand how bad I been wanting you. Just let me eat it, and that's it. You don't have to do nothing else after that if you don't want to," he offered as he lightly tugged on my jeans.

Should I? Julius would never know. Maybe this will get him off my back for a while, I thought.

He bit his lip and smiled as he tugged on my jeans some more. He finally pulled them all the way off and then reached up for my panties. My heart started to speed up as I wondered if I should stop him. Julius cheated on me plenty of times; this one thing isn't as bad. *No Natalia, two wrongs don't make a right. Julius has changed!* My thoughts switched back and forth. I felt like I had an angel on one shoulder and the devil on the other.

"Stop Marlon," I finally spoke up.

"WHAT THE FUCK!!" he yelled so loud I felt it in my chest.

I quickly pulled my panties up and then grabbed my jeans. Marlon dropped his head in his hands and started breathing heavily as I slid my jeans up.

"I have to go," I said as I grabbed my purse and keys.

"Wait, Natalia. I'm sorry. If you need time, that's cool," he said in a calmer tone. "I love you enough to wait."

"Okay, thank you," I smiled and kissed his lips.

He wrapped his arms around my waist and dipped his tongue in my mouth. I had forgotten how bad of a kisser he was until now. I abruptly pulled back when my phone started to ring, we both looked down at it and Julius' name flashed across.

"I have to go," I repeated.

"You bet not be going to see him Nat," he glared at me.

"No, I-I'm going to check on my kids," I smiled uncomfortably. I didn't like the fact that he felt he could tell me when to see Julius.

"Good," he nodded and pecked my lips.

I walked out of his apartment and once I got far enough, I called Julius back. I was so on edge from all this cheating I was doing that I didn't even know whom exactly I was cheating on. I mean, technically I was married to Julius, but we broke up and Marlon became my boyfriend. But like Julius said, we're married, we can't just break up.

"Why you didn't answer the first time Natalia?" Julius said into the phone.

"I didn't get to it fast enough," I said looking around as if he was watching me.

"Whatever, where you at?" he asked.

"I-I'm with Lucy," I stammered hoping he hadn't talked to her. I knew he hadn't, but that's just how paranoid I was. I wasn't built to cheat at all.

"Come home, I want some midday," he replied sounding like he was smiling.

"Okay," I chuckled.

I sped home, happy that Julius had no idea where I really was. He may revert to his old ways if he knew I was at another guy's home, who thought I was his girlfriend. As soon as I walked into the house, I checked on Winnie and the babies to make sure everything was fine.

"I already did that," Julius said pulling my arm, and picking me up bridal style.

"Ouch," I whined because I was so sore.

He carried me up the stairs into our bedroom and laid me down, then immediately climbed between my legs. He removed my shirt and unhooked my bra to suck my nipples. Once he finished sucking, licking and biting my nipples, I was ready and so was he. He kissed down my stomach and then suddenly stopped.

"Why the fuck are your pants unzipped?" he glared down at me.

I pressed my chin into my chest to look down and yep, my jeans were unzipped. I buttoned them but forgot to zip. *Prepare for the worst Natalia,* I said to myself, waiting for a slap or punch.

"Answer me! You was out fucking another nigga?" Julius yelled making me jump.

"No, I... I uh... They were-"

"Get it out Natalia. I'm giving you a fucking chance to explain to me why your damn pants are unzipped."

"Okay! I went to see Marlon and he wanted to do it. He was trying to take my pants off but I stopped him. When I rushed out, I guess I forgot to zip my pants," I cried.

He stared at me with an angry scowl and then plopped down next to me. He intertwined his fingers in his lap and then threw his head back to let out a deep sigh. I stood up and pulled my jeans down and off. I removed my panties as well, so that I was naked at this point. I stood between his legs, pulled off his shirt and then tugged down his sweats and boxers.

"Natalia, get off me," he said.

I ignored him and took his eleven inches into my mouth. I sucked on the tip and then deep throated him like I had never done before. My saliva was rushing down his shaft, as my mouth slid up and down it.

"Shit, ahhhh fuck," he moaned as his dick hardened.

He shot his seeds down my throat and I licked his dick clean. I stood up and his face was still angry. I climbed into his lap and forced his thick shaft inside me. It was slightly painful due to his size and me still being sore down there, but I couldn't worry about that. I needed to make up what I had just done to my husband. I wrapped my arms tightly around his neck and pressed my soft body against his hard one. I held tightly onto him, as I bounced slowly on his dick, giving my vagina a chance to adjust.

"Ahhh, Juuu," I whimpered knowing I would be cumming soon.

Finally, he wrapped his arms around my petite frame, hugging me tightly, as I bounced on his dick slowly. I pulled away just enough to look down into his face and suck on his lips. He lifted my legs onto his forearms, to give himself more access to my opening.

"I love you Julius. You know I wouldn't give your pussy away," I moaned as we stared into each other's eyes. "Uhhh," I moaned as I felt myself cum on his dick.

Julius flipped me onto my back and lightly grabbed onto my neck.

He pumped into me fast and hard, hitting my spot constantly. He then grabbed my hands and pinned them above my head tightly.

"Break it off with that nigga," he said staring into my eyes, as he slowed down his pumps. I simply nodded to say okay.

Natalia was really pushing my buttons. I didn't know if I was more upset at the fact that she was still fucking around with that nigga Julius, or that she expected me to believe all the lies she fed me.

The only reason I was accepting her bullshit was because I loved that girl. I didn't care that she had two kids with another man; I wanted her. She was so sexy to me. She was averaged height, with a smooth, honey butter complexion. Her full lips were always looking kissable and her smile was the prettiest one I'd ever seen. Although she wasn't thick, her small body still had some shape to it. Her long chestnut brown hair matched perfectly with her skin tone. I've never wanted to make love to somebody so damn bad.

Tonight, we were going out to dinner and I was hoping she would let me fuck. I was gonna be patient with her and maybe even get a couple drinks into her system. Maybe if she was drunk enough, she would slide up out them panties. She may regret it in the morning, but at least I would finally get a taste of that pussy. I didn't give a fuck how I got the pussy at this point, as long as I got it. Even raping her didn't sound too bad.

We were sitting at the table inside Red Lobster, and I just stared at her as she looked over the menu. She had on a black tube dress, her favorite, and some stilettos. Those tube dresses fit her small, shapely frame so perfect. This one in particular was cut out on the sides, so you could see the side of her small perky breasts, and unfortunately that tattoo of that nigga's name.

"What?" she frowned and fixed her messy curly bun. Her bracelets jingled as she moved her arms around.

"Nothing, just admiring what I see," I replied licking my lips and she smiled.

As if my eyes were playing tricks on me, I saw Julius walking in the restaurant and right over to our table. I really didn't want any problems with him because I knew he was crazy. That fight in the club was still fresh in my mind. I didn't like the fact that one minute we were fighting and the next, some random muthafucka was slapping me awake. Niggas said he was crazy about Natalia and that's why I tried to make sure they were done.

"Natalia, let's go!" he boomed.

"Julius," she said grabbing her purse to get up.

"Wait, I thought you and him weren't together anymore?" I frowned. I didn't want to speak up, but Natalia was mine. I had plans on sliding up in that tonight and an ass whooping was worth it right now.

She just stood up and led Julius out the restaurant by his hand. I waited until they got outside and then got up to follow them. I stood two cars away so that they wouldn't see me, but I could see and hear them. It was dark outside, so I really didn't have to worry about them seeing me anyway. I wanted to find out what she was feeding this nigga.

"What the fuck you doing out here with this nigga Nat? You gone make me kill homie!" Julius yelled. I bucked my eyes because I didn't know he was tryna kill a brother.

"I'm tryna let him down easy," she said cupping his face. *This bitch is for real shady,* I thought and shook my head. I just knew she was telling me one thing and then telling him another. I guess she thought she was some type of player. I didn't care; if she was gone still give me some, then that's all that mattered. I did, however, love her little sneaky ass. It was just something about her.

She planted a couple kisses on his lips and then he pulled on the handle to her backseat door. She climbed in and he went in after her. *Wow, she's just gone leave,* I thought. Until I realized they were still in the backseat. I quietly walked over to where I could see a little into her backseat since she had no damn tint. This girl was fucking this nigga, right here in the parking lot, while I was supposedly waiting on her in the restaurant. To make matters worse, she was telling me she wasn't ready to sleep with anyone. I became enraged as I watched her bounce on his dick and then him throw his head back in pleasure. That was supposed to be my dick she was bouncing on tonight.

I went back into the restaurant just to see if she would even let me know anything. After about thirty fucking minutes, she came walking in with a fucking hickey on her neck. If I didn't know for sure that Julius would fuck me up and murder me for putting my hands on her, I would've knocked the shit out of her for doing me so damn dirty. Did she really fuck another nigga while on a date with me? What has my life come to?

"Uh Marlon, I'm gonna go," she said not even bothering to sit down.

"Don't leave 'cause of him," I said, playing along with her stupid ass games.

"No, it's not about him. I-I just got to go," she said and turned around to leave.

I followed after her, after a couple seconds had passed and she was following her bitch ass husband out of the parking lot. It was cool though, because I already had me a little bitch on the side that I was feeling. I decided to shoot her text since my night had suddenly opened up.

Me: You up babe?
Lucy: Yeah, I am.

JULIUS

Today, I was meeting with an old associate of mine that I worked with while back in Indiana named Chico. He worked for Hugo like myself, but wanted to get up with me. That was cool, but I needed to know why all of a sudden he wanted to come this way. Aside from me, Chico was one of Hugo's biggest moneymakers, so I knew he wouldn't like him coming to work for me. I really didn't care because our relationship had soured long ago. Any loyalty I had to Hugo left the building that night in California.

"What's up man?" Chico smiled as he sat across from my desk.

"You tell me. You sure you wanna come over here?" I frowned. He needed to be leaving for the right reasons. If he was just ditching Hugo for some dumb shit, then that would show me he had no loyalty.

"I'm positive," he nodded.

"Why? What's going on back in Indianapolis?" I inquired.

"Hugo ain't doing shit. We barely moving weight and the product just ain't up to par. I let that nigga know if he didn't find a better plug, I was gone," he replied shaking his head.

"So the streets are drying up?" I asked surprised.

"Drier than the damn Sahara my nigga. I ain't the only one looking for work elsewhere," he said and I nodded. "So what's up Julius, you gone put me on?" he quizzed.

"I don't know man. I don't know if you really ready to make an enemy out of Hugo," I said.

"Man, fuck Hugo. You know you and I were the only ones that wasn't scared of that nigga," he spat.

"True. I don't need you to be scared of me either, but I need you to respect me as your boss. Is that something you can do? Can you get used to working under me instead of beside me?" I questioned to make sure.

I didn't need any salty ass niggas in my operation. Muthafuckas always felt like since they worked beside you at one point in life, you didn't deserve to give them orders. If that's how Chico felt, then there would be no point in him working for me. Plus, Chico knew I was in the game years before he ever was, so he should have no problem with me being his boss.

"I ain't tripping off that. It's too much work being the boss, so please take the lead," he smiled and threw his hands up in mock surrender.

"Cool, good to hear. So right now, I want you to collect and double check the money from the traps for me. If any of it is short, I need you to make sure it's found. If niggas is stuttering and stammering as to where it is, handle ya business. You know when a nigga is doing dirt," I said. "If you can't find the money or present me with the nigga responsible, then you and I are gonna have some problems," I added.

I trusted Chico, which is why I gave him such a high position. Chico could read a nigga in thirty seconds and let you know if he was a snake or not. He'd been telling me that Menzo was a snake for the longest, and he was right.

"No problem boss," he smiled and nodded. I couldn't say that I wasn't happy to have Chico on my team. He was a hard worker and could work any position that you needed him to.

"So how's life my nigga? You married? Kids?" I inquired.

"Nah, not yet. Maybe it'll be some better girls down South. But I heard you married your girl from Indianapolis," he replied.

"Natalia. Yeah man, I had to. She had a nigga gone in the head so I knew it was right," I half joked, and we both laughed.

"Hell yeah nigga, if she got you ready to body niggas and acting psycho, she's the one," he chuckled.

"Who the fuck you telling?" I shook my head thinking about my wife. I loved the fuck out of her and to make shit worse, the pussy was just indescribable. It should be illegal to have some shit like that between your legs.

"What happened to old girl with the red hair?" Chico asked referring to Bianca's old coo-coo ass.

"Man, that bitch faked a pregnancy on me. Had me put in jail, all kinds of shit."

"What? That whole time y'all dated she never seemed like the type," he frowned.

"Those are the ones I guess. Her honey nut ass is in jail now though," I said shaking my head.

"What you doing to these hoes out here, bruh?" he asked laughing his ass off.

"Shit, I don't even know. I'm still trying to figure that shit out," I replied shaking my head.

"Yeah, well maybe you can introduce me to a chick down here. I need me a little wifey to hold me down like you got," he smiled.

"They're hard to find, but you'll know it when you find it," I nodded, and so did he.

I was doing laundry and helping Winnie out around the house. I was trying to stay busy because whenever I got bored, I would end up talking to Marlon. I hated to use him but he let me. If he wouldn't allow me to walk all over him and use him when Julius hurt me, I wouldn't do it. After what happened at Red Lobster that night, you would think he would be off me, but nope. He let a couple days go by and then he was blowing up my phone again. These days, I hated to look at my phone around Julius because it would be about one hundred notifications from Marlon's ass.

I was tired, so I carried the basket of Jackson and Harmony's onesies and clothes upstairs. I was gonna fold them in the bedroom, where I could relax and watch TV. As I was folding clothes, Julius' phone kept buzzing. I took a deep breath and told myself to ignore it. It buzzed again and I glanced at the screen. Someone named Franceska had texted him, the same girl from when I was pregnant with Jackson. I instantly got a flashback of watching him get dressed to leave and go see her. My stomach became queasy at the thought.

I paused to make sure the shower was still running before I picked it up and slid it open. She'd sent a picture of herself in lingerie. *Lisa?* I thought. Who was this hoe? She told me her name was Lisa when she tried to work for me, but Julius had her stored as Franceska. She was really thick and it made me feel uncomfortable with my small frame. I had nice thighs, a plump ass, small round perky boobs and a flat stomach, but my hips weren't as wide as hers. Her boobs were huge and her butt was its own person. I was tired of this bitch coming for my man. I knew I should've beat her ass that day she popped up at my house tryna tell me she was still fucking with Julius.

I got up and walked into the bathroom where Julius was showering. I waited and waited until he finally cut the water off. He stepped out and his body was so sexy. His short fade was wet and I almost forgot why I was mad at him. My mouth watered at his dick swinging. It wasn't hard but it was still an okay size. I wanted to get in the shower and pull him back with me. I was convinced my husband was the sexiest man in America.

"You scared me babe," he chuckled and then wrapped his towel around his waist.

"What is she sending this for?" I asked holding his phone up. He exhaled heavily before speaking.

"I don't know. Ain't like I asked for it," he frowned. "Scroll the fuck up and you'll see," he frowned.

"But you must be telling her something to where she thinks this is okay. You have a wife and two babies!" I yelled getting angry.

"I got a wife, who's running her ass around town with another nigga all the fucking time. I told you to break it off with that nigga!" he yelled back at me. "You want me to murder this nigga? Is that what I have to do to keep you off his dick?" he frowned.

"I ain't ever been on his dick! And I told you that I was breaking it off at that dinner you saw me at!" I shouted.

"You expect me to believe that Natalia?" he asked as he walked closer to me. I stood up because I was scared he would hit me. Even though it'd been forever since he had done so, I was still a little worried when he became angry.

"It's the truth Julius," I replied in a calmer tone.

"How you think that makes me look, when you out with this nigga all the fucking time. You wanna be with him Natalia?" he said getting super close to me.

"No, I want you."

"No, I think you want his ass," he replied and walked out the bathroom.

I turned and followed right after his ass. He closed the bedroom door and then dropped his towel to put his boxers on. I walked over to him and hugged him tightly. He paused for a second and then finally reciprocated the hug.

"I love you Julius. Only you," I whispered.

He lifted me up and I wrapped my legs around his waist. He reached under my dress and pulled my panties to the side from behind. He brought me down onto his long, thick, shaft and started to pump into me slowly.

"Tell me who this pussy belongs to," he demanded to know.

"Julius Tate," I moaned.

He stood there, holding me up as if I was a feather, and brought me up and down onto his dick. I looked over at the mirror and watched how good our bodies looked together. I loved this man and I just needed to let Marlon go. I couldn't keep holding on to a guy I didn't want, just in case the man I loved messed up.

JULIUS

Natalia really had the game fucked up and twisted if she thought she could constantly fuck up and just throw some pussy my way to make me forget about it. Either she was gone stop talking to this nigga altogether, or I was gone start fucking around on her too. Ain't no way I was gone sit here and be all faithful and shit, while she went out on dates. Honestly, I was worried that she was in love with this nigga or something. Why couldn't she leave him alone? The more I thought about it, the angrier I became.

Today, I made her ass think that I was leaving to take care of some business. I knew when I left the house, she would be on the phone with that nigga to pass the time. I just needed to catch her ass in the act. I was sitting in the garage waiting, when I finally decided to creep back up in the house. I walked up the stairs and saw that our bedroom door was closed. I put my ear to the door and sure enough, Ms. Natalia was on the phone. I wanted to listen for a bit, because I wanted to make sure she was actually talking to *his* ass.

"No, I can't see you anymore," she said. "I don't want to use you anymore Marlon," she added. *She bet not have been using him for no dick.* I said to myself.

I twisted the knob and slowly walked into the room. Her eyes got big as saucers as she slid the phone down her face. She pressed the end button and I stared at her with my arms folded.

"What the fuck you doing?" I asked.

"I was talking to-to Lucy," she lied.

"Really? Because I heard you mention Marlon's name," I replied. She just stared up at me with nothing to say. "Fuck this. I tried to be faithful to you, but I'm starting to see that's not what you want," I said.

"Yes it is Ju! I was telling him it's over," she cried.

"Over? It should've never fucking started! Once I put that ring on your finger, any other nigga should've been irrelevant!" I yelled.

"They are!" she hollered.

"Then what's up? Why are you constantly talking to this muthafucka? I've told you on countless occasions to stop fucking around with him," I said through gritted teeth.

She was so lucky that my love for her wouldn't allow me to hit her anymore. I loved her little ass more than anything, and sometimes I hated it. I was starting to think that maybe I loved her way more than she loved me.

"I know Julius and I'm not gonna talk to him anymore baby, I promise!" she said with tears running down her beautiful face.

"I don't believe you. You've said that shit one-hundred damn times and every time was a lie. I'm gone head out for a bit," I said.

"Where are you going?" she asked finally standing up off the bed.

"Out, maybe I'll go on a date or two," I said.

She frowned up her cute little face and pushed me with all her little might. I barely moved and she pushed me again. She slapped me hard as hell and then pushed me back again. I reached to grab her, but she darted away towards the door. I grabbed her from behind and carried her crazy ass to the bed. I climbed on her back and bit her shoulder from behind.

"Ahhh!" she screamed.

I reached under her skirt and pulled her thong down roughly. I pulled my dick out and then slid it into her sopping wet walls.

"Is this what you want? You want it rough?" I asked as I grabbed a fistful of her hair, while ramming my dick into her.

I turned her face to the side and sucked her sexy lips. I dipped my tongue into her mouth and she reached around to cup my head. I slid my hand down the front of her body and played with her swollen clit, as she spread her legs to give me more access. Power of the pussy; she had me again.

"I'm about to cum daddy," she moaned as I tugged on her lip. "Ahhh, uhhhh!" she cried out, as I tore her shit up.

"Ahhh fuck," I grunted. Natalia was the only woman that could make me moan like a bitch.

I sped up my pace, feeling my nut rise and her pussy get wetter. I looked down at her smooth ass bouncing and busted all in her walls. She jerked a bit from cumming herself and then panted out of breath.

"You like that rough shit, with yo' freaky ass," I smirked.

She turned around and sat up to suck my dick. Her award winning pussy and head wasn't gone work this time though. If she wanted to play with muthafuckas' hearts, so could I.

"**W**hy do you take so long to call me?" Franceska asked as we sat in her living room.

I knew I should've had my ass at home, but fuck that. I didn't want to admit to myself that Natalia had a hold on me and no other bitch could compare. I wanted to be the old Julius again, but I was having a hard time doing so.

"I be busy," I shrugged. Shit, after I got out of jail for those drugs, her ass had disappeared for a bit too, so she shouldn't be talking.

"So you and Natalia are really done for good?" she smiled.

"Yeah, we a wrap," I lied. Natalia and I would never be done. I could be married to a new bitch and Natalia would still be number one.

"So where does that leave me?" she cheesed big as hell.

"We just chilling like usual," I frowned. I was getting frustrated with all her damn questions. She stayed tryna make something out of absolutely nothing at all.

"You don't even wanna try and see where this could go?" she asked with a concerned expression.

"I guess we could try something out," I replied as I eyed her thick ass body. I didn't mean anything that I was saying. All I wanted was some pussy and head. I would tell her anything right about now to shut her up and get her up out them panties.

"For real babe?" she questioned excitedly.

"Yup," I nodded and tucked in my lips. "Now come take care of me," I said releasing my dick for some head.

NATALIA

Julius left out after we had sex and hasn't been back. It's been a week now and he hasn't answered any of my calls or texts either. It was just like when we first met, so I knew he was up to no good. This is the exact reason why I tried to keep Marlon around. I knew sooner or later, Julius would revert back to his old ways. It was like we could never be happy for more than a couple months.

Although Julius and my relationship was on the rocks, I still needed to let Marlon go. I had no interest in being with him and I had still been sleeping with Julius the whole time we were "together." I couldn't even bring myself to have sex with him, so I knew I couldn't be with him. Don't get me wrong, Marlon was a really nice looking guy, but my heart and mind was with Julius Tate. It had been that way ever since that night in CVS.

I decided to just drop by Marlon's on my way to the grocery store, since he wasn't responding this morning. I needed to tell him this face to face anyway. He deserved that much for how badly I'd been treating him.

I pulled up to his apartment complex and headed inside. I wasn't nervous at all; I was actually feeling good that I'd gotten enough courage to let him go. It would be a weight off my shoulders having him out of my life. I know that sounds mean, but it was true. I was tired of the constant phone calls, texts, lies and excuses I had to give to keep him from between my legs.

I walked up his stairs and then knocked on his door lightly. No one answered so I knocked a couple more times. I heard rustling and then someone finally came to the door to open it.

"What's up?" Marlon asked. He opened the door only enough to peek his head out. *Okay?*

"Can we talk?" I smiled.

"About what?" he frowned.

"Can I come in first?" I asked.

"Nah, it's not a good time babe," he replied.

"Okay, well I think it's best that we don't talk anymore. Not even as friends. I'm married and that's who I want to be with," I stated.

"I asked yo' lying ass if you wanted to be with him!" he yelled angrily. "You think it's that easy Natalia? You think you can just walk up to me say you done? Nah ma, you in too fucking deep now and you gone have to woman up and deal with me." He nodded like what he was saying was factual.

"Babe, who is at the door?" I heard a familiar voice yell.

"Lucy!" I yelled back, pushing the door open.

Marlon stumbled back as I walked through the house in search of her. I went to the bedroom and there she was under the covers. Her hair was disheveled, and she was naked as the day she was born. Had he been fucking her the whole time? Why was she always trying to sleep with my niggas?

"Natalia? What are you doing here?" she frowned and held the sheet up over her body.

"What the fuck are *you* doing here?" I shouted.

"Look Natalia, go somewhere with that bullshit," Marlon frowned and walked into the room.

"Wait, you still messing with Marlon?" Lucy frowned in confusion.

"Wow, so you fucking my ex best friend and trying to have sex with me?" I said to Marlon. "You are such a fucking dog!"

"Really Natalia? You fucked your husband in the parking lot while we were on a date!" he hollered. I didn't say anything in response. "Yeah, you thought I didn't know, ma?" he chuckled. "Spitting all this bullshit to me about how you ain't ready for sex with nobody, but you busting it open for ole thug passion," he panted with his fists balled up.

"I sure did! That's the only nigga that will ever get some too! You thirsty ass bitch!" I yelled back to him.

"Oh, I'll show you thirsty ma. You just watch and see," he nodded.

"Natalia, I swear I didn't know that you guys were even like that," Lucy pleaded. "He never mentioned you. I thought you guys didn't talk to one another past the night at the club," she added while shaking her head.

I just shook my head as well and turned to leave. Marlon followed after me and pulled on my arm, but I snatched it back and headed out. I no longer felt bad for using his whack ass. I couldn't believe I messed up my marriage over a nigga like him.

JULIUS

I hadn't spoken to Natalia in about two weeks and to be honest, I was starting to feel sick. I hated that I loved her ass so much, but it was what it was. Like a dumb ass, I had Franceska thinking we were a couple or some shit. She stayed blowing me up and then had the nerve to try and fucking check me when I would go days without speaking to her. She was really doing the most, and it was starting to make me hate her ass as much as I hated Bianca. I should've just stayed to myself instead of running up in her just because my wife pissed me off. Now I possibly had another psycho bitch on my hands.

I was chilling in the old condo, when I heard a key in the door. I already knew who it was, cause only two other people had keys to the house; Winnie and Natalia. Just as I suspected, Natalia walked in and smiled when she saw me. I shook my head at her and set my Jack Daniels down on the coffee table. She removed her jacket and ran over to me. She rushed into my lap, straddling me, and hugged me tight. I inhaled her scent, which I loved. She always smelled like some kind of sweet sugar. I missed her so damn much, but I couldn't let her know that.

"Where have you been?" she asked looking down into my face.

"Doing my thang," I replied nonchalantly.

She stared down into my eyes and then kissed my lips softly. I dipped my tongue into her mouth and sucked on her soft ass lips. I was hugging her body tight as hell because I never wanted to let her go. I loved this girl man. *Fuck.*

"Why you have to play games, ma?" I asked in between kisses. I was sounding like a bitch and I needed to snap out of it.

"I'm not Ju. I love you, I don't deal with Marlon anymore," she replied as she cupped my face. "I want you to come home," she added.

She pulled off the dress she had on, and all she had on were crotch-less panties. She reached down into my sweats and started to stroke my dick. When did she become such a seductress? Or maybe this only worked on me. I better had been the only nigga she was trying this on.

"I can't," I said unconvincingly.

"Why?" she frowned as she still stroked my dick.

She finally pulled it out and smiled because it was rock hard. She got up and then slid down on it.

"Ooohhhhh," we both moaned together.

"Because, I'm mad at you Natalia. I don't know if I even want to be with you anymore," I replied, referring to her question earlier.

She stopped slowly bouncing on my dick and stared into my eyes. She then frowned in confusion, as her pussy throbbed around my dick.

"What? Why Julius? I didn't even do anything with him!" she started to cry and then slid my dick out of her.

"Why you stop?" I asked. I still wanted to fuck her, regardless of me being mad.

"I'm not in the mood to have sex with you anymore," she replied, folding her arms over her chest.

"You were cheating emotionally, Natalia, and that's worse than physical," I replied wiping her tears.

"No I didn't! I never cared about him!" she said breaking down.

"I told you time and time again to leave that nigga alone and you acted like you just couldn't let him go. You must've fallen for the nigga." I finally spoke my mind and it hurt to hear my own words.

"I did not fall for him Julius! I only kept him because I thought you would cheat on me again and I wanted to have someone for when you did," she cried even harder. She just pissed me off even more with that bullshit she just said.

"I told you that I wasn't gone fuck around on you anymore. You acted like you believed me. If you can't even trust what I tell you, then why the fuck are you with me?" I frowned.

I never knew how niggas could only love and want to be with one female, until I met Natalia. She was the only one I wanted, and I meant it when I said I would never cheat or hit her again. For her to not even believe me was fucked up in my opinion. I was really trying and I was succeeding too. Now, here she is waiting in the background for me to fuck up.

"It's hard to explain Julius, just please come back home. I need you, daddy. Jackson and Harmony need you," she said sniffling. She was so pretty. She grabbed my face and planted kisses on my lips back to back. "I love you Ju. Please," she added.

"I love you too, ma. But right now I can't do this with you. I need some time to think," I said.

She paused and then got off my lap. She grabbed her purse and jacket and left the house. I knew I wanted to be with her, but I needed to teach her ass a lesson. If she was gone be with me, then she needed to be with me only. I didn't have time for a hoe as a wife.

NATALIA

2 WEEKS LATER

I hated Julius so damn much right now. He knew nothing happened between Marlon and I, yet he was punishing me. Emotionally cheating? Yeah right. I had absolutely no feelings for Marlon. Any ones that I did have, completely went away the more we hung together. I just wish I could go back in time and break it off with Marlon when I first started to. I would have my husband back, and my family would be complete. I wouldn't be laid up every night, crying myself to sleep.

"Goodnight cutie," I smiled as I laid Harmony down into her crib. She was so beautiful and a perfect mixture of Julius and I.

I walked out of her room and into Jackson's. He was still playing with his toys and it was already 10pm. I picked him up out of his crib to get him dressed for bed, so that I could go to my room and sulk. As I was changing him into his pajamas, his room door opened. I turned around and saw Julius standing in the doorway.

"What do you want?" I asked with as much attitude as I could muster up.

"You," he said flashing his perfect smile.

"Too bad," I replied as I picked Jackson up and put him in the crib.

I cut the light off in his room, and then walked past Julius out the door. Once I got into the bedroom, I cut the light off and started to channel surf. A couple minutes passed and then Julius entered the bedroom smiling again. What the fuck was so funny? I ignored him and continued to look for something good to watch. He walked over to me and took the remote out my hand while biting his lip.

"What do you want?" I asked as he started to undress.

"I just told you," he replied as he threw the covers off my lap.

He reached up under my gown and pulled my panties off quickly. He pulled my gown up over my head and admired my body for a couple seconds. He kissed down my toned stomach, until he reached my hotbox and kissed it slowly and softly.

"Look at this shit," he said as he slowly licked between the slit. "You taste so good Natalia," he moaned, as he sucked and flicked his tongue over my clit. "I love eating this baby," he added.

"Ahhh Juuuu, damn," I purred as he spread my legs some more.

He locked his mouth onto my clit and sucked the life out of it. I rubbed the back of his head, as he performed his magic between my legs. I released all over his lips and he licked up every bit as I shivered. He stood up, got on top of me between my legs and rubbed his hands over my vagina.

"You're so wet. You always get so wet for me," he commented, as he looked down at his hand against my pussy.

"Juuu, put it in," I begged.

An evil smile crept across his face, as he gently tapped his dick against my kitten. He was driving me crazy and he knew it.

"Beg for it," he demanded.

"Please Ju," I begged some more as I scooted closer to it. He smiled and bit his lip at the sound of me pleading.

"This better still be exclusive," he said as he positioned his head at my opening.

"It is," I moaned as I felt him plunge inside me.

He wrapped both arms around my torso and hugged me tightly, as he pumped into my wetness. I draped my arms over his shoulders and hugged him back, as we kissed passionately. I was so in love with him, that it didn't make any sense.

"I love you so much Nat. You make a nigga crazy," he said as he pumped me slowly.

"I love you more Ju. I promise… only you, daddy," I whispered into his mouth.

He cupped my small breasts and sucked on the nipples, as I released on his dick. It was raining lightly outside and the sound was so soothing, as we continued to make love to one another. I felt so high when I was with him and it was no better feeling.

JULIUS

"So what's going on?" I asked my boys Dash and Leese. They called me and let me know they had something to tell me and that it was important. I wondered what it could be, but came up short. I didn't have beef with anybody and if any of my traps were fucked with, I would've known about it already.

"That nigga Hugo is gunning for you," Dash replied.

"What? Why? That beef we had about the connect was over and done with I thought," I frowned. *That old muthafucka must've been bored at home,* I thought.

This nigga couldn't possibly still be mad about me getting Bart as a connect. The shit happened almost a year ago, so there had to be another reason as to why he felt the need to be "gunning for me" now. Regardless of the reason, I wasn't scared of his ass.

"It's about Chico," Leese said.

"Wait, why don't he take that beef up with Chico?" I asked no one in particular. Hugo was probably waiting for a fucking reason to come for me and now he had one.

"I have no idea. All I know is that the streets know he's looking for you," Leese replied.

This was almost laughable right now. Hugo had the nerve to be after me because one of his workers left? Ain't like I kidnapped the nigga. That muthafucka decided to come work for me using his own damn brain. I had nothing to do with that shit.

"So any specifics?" I asked.

"Not really. They just saying he gone kill yo' ass," Dash replied.

"Wow," I said laughing.

This shit was actually comical because nobody was scared of Hugo's ass. If he did try to kill me, he'd better make sure I was dead because I would dedicate the rest of my days to finding him. Hugo knew I was no bitch nigga and that I didn't deal with threats too well, so that's why this whole thing was a secret. Hugo was looking more and more like a bitch to me as time went on.

"Somebody call Chico for me," I said and Leese nodded.

Chico had finally arrived to my office and I had a couple questions for his ass. I was wondering if he mentioned something to Hugo that would make him think I had something to do with his decision to bounce on his ass. I never knew Chico to be a snake but shit, you never knew these days. Ain't like he was one of my day ones.

"What's up player?" Chico smiled as he sat down.

"Your man, Hugo has put a price on my head," I replied and stared him down to see if he made any nervous movements.

"Damn, for what?" he frowned.

"For you. What did you tell him before you left? Please don't lie to me Chico," I replied and squinted my eyes as if it would make me see better.

"I just told that nigga that if he didn't shape up, I was gone come work for you," he smiled.

"Well that explains it," I said shaking my head. Chico knew all too well that Hugo and I had a bad relationship because of the connect. Of course the nigga was gonna retaliate if he knew Chico went to work for me.

"Aye man, I can help you out with getting at this nigga. You know it ain't nothing for me," he said shaking his head.

"Nah, you good right now. Hugo is a bitch. If he comes for me, he better make sure he kills me because I'm gone come back one-hundred times harder on that nigga," I said looking off into the distance.

Hugo had no idea who he was fucking with. I wasn't that same little stick up kid that he put on. I was a grown ass man who feared nothing in this world but God. I wasn't even scared of death. If his old ass wanted to go to war, I was gone give him a run for his fucking money.

I'll tell you this though, he better not come for my wife or kids because that will get him in a whole world of trouble. Hugo has been known in the past to fuck with people's families when they pissed him off. Those niggas were scary though. I'm a different breed and he ain't used to having enemies like me. Too bad he doesn't have anybody with enough balls to warn him that this is not something he wants. For now, I wasn't gone worry too much about it though. I was gone wait and see if he actually made a move. If he did, no matter how big or small, I would be out for blood… his blood.

2 WEEKS LATER

Julius' dumb ass left his iPad here, so all his little texts were coming through on it. I kept it next to me and read every single one that bitch Franceska was sending. Tonight his dumb ass was gonna meet her at his club but little did he know, so the fuck was I. Julius was my husband and if that stupid hoe thought she was gonna just slide in after all I've done, she had another thing coming. I could bet my life that tonight Julius Tate was coming home with me.

After I fed my babies and put them to bed, I went to get dressed for the night. I chose a red skirt that was nice and short, with a matching red tube top. I put on an arm bracelet, some earrings and of course, my promise chain. I let my brown curly hair hang loose and I was ready to go. I smiled at myself in the full-length mirror 'cause I knew Julius was either gonna have a fit or be turned on. Either way, I wouldn't go unnoticed tonight.

"Damn you look good bitch," Paula smiled once she got into my car.

"That's the plan," I smiled.

I looked at my iPhone and saw it was 10pm, so I knew that Julius and that Franceska hoe were already there. We pulled up to Club Rissani and it was a long line outside. I knew it was gone be live as hell tonight for sure; even better. Paula and I exited the car and headed straight up to the front. There was no way I was about to wait in line when my husband owned this damn club.

"You look nice tonight Natalia," the bouncer said as he licked his lips. He didn't ask any questions or give me any grief. He simply removed the rope, with that ugly ass smile plastered on his face.

"Thank you," I grinned and walked into the club.

Just as I expected, the club was packed wall to fucking wall. Everybody was drinking, socializing and freaking on one another on the dance floor. I scanned the VIP booths looking for Julius. I hoped he was in one of them because if not, then that meant he was probably in his office fucking that stupid bitch. Just as I was starting to get worried, I spotted him chilling with that hoe in his lap. My heart started to hurt, but I refused to let it show on my face.

"Show time," I smiled at Paula and she smiled back.

We walked up to the booth next to Julius and his homeboys, and it was full of some boss looking ass dudes. All I did was walk up and flash my smile, and these niggas let me into their VIP. I strutted past them knowing I looked good as hell. The babies I had gave me a little more in all the right areas. I was still small but just had a little more to give.

"You want a drink sexy?" one of the guys asked me.

"Yes please," I replied in a flirty tone and Paula chuckled.

He poured me a drink and gave one to Paula as well. I hadn't drunk in so long, so it felt like pure rubbing alcohol going down my throat. After a couple drinks, I started to loosen up and the guy that gave me a drink was flirting with me a lot. I looked over and saw Julius was still playing boyfriend and girlfriend with that bitch.

"I'm Up," by Omarion came on, and the guy pulled me into his lap for a dance. *Fuck it,* I told myself. I started grinding in his lap and twerking my ass as he held onto my waist.

"You sexy as hell, ma," the guy commented, as he rubbed his big hand on my flat stomach.

Like fucking clockwork, I heard some commotion and then

spotted Julius storming past a group of niggas to get to me. He snatched me up by my arm with the quickness.

"Fuck you doing Natalia!" he yelled.

"Aye nigga! We was dancing!" the guy shouted, standing up.

"Nigga, sit yo' muthafuckin' ass down before I fuck you up. My wife is off limits, aight!" Julius hollered back getting in his face. All the guys' homeboys were surrounding him, yet Julius refused to back down. That was the type of guy he was though, never one to back down from anyone or anything. "Now I suggest y'all sit the fuck back down and continue to enjoy y'all night," Julius added and then snatched me out the VIP.

He led me to the back and when I looked over my shoulder, I saw Franceska following in the distance. We finally reached his office and he slammed the door shut. We stared at each other for a little bit and I could see he was angry as fuck. He was so sexy, especially when he clenched his jaw and scowled like that.

"That's what the fuck you do now?" he asked with his fists balled up.

"I don't see why you care. Looks like you have a girlfriend already," I said feeling hurt.

"Don't you ever do no shit like that again," he replied breathing heavily.

"I'm single. I can dance on and fuck whomever I want. Just like you," I smiled and then headed towards the door.

Julius grabbed my arm and pulled me back. He rushed me into the wall and towered over me.

"You not fucking single, you my damn wife."

"I'm not your wife! You had that slut all in your lap while I'm at home missing you," I cried almost.

He grabbed my face and dipped his tongue in my mouth. We were so caught up in our kiss that we didn't realize someone had walked in. That someone was Franceska's ass.

"Julius!" she yelled.

"Aye Franceska, I'm busy," Julius replied.

"Busy cheating on me!" she screamed.

"He ain't cheating on you, I'm his wife! You a fucking nobody bitch!" I yelled back.

"Natalia relax," Julius said.

"No, I'm not relaxing. Either you leaving with me right now or you can stay here with her and divorce me," I said giving him an ultimatum. I was done with his fucking games.

"Aight, go wait for me in the car," he huffed.

"For real Julius?" Franceska yelled.

"No," I said folding my arms. I wasn't about to wait in the car so he could dick this bitch down. Whatever she got from him up until this point, was the last she was gonna get.

Julius exhaled heavily and then grabbed my hand in his. Franceska shook her head at him as tears rushed down her trashy face. She ran out, being dramatic as fuck, and Julius and I headed out his office.

"Gimme a kiss with yo' crazy ass," he grinned down at me. I smiled back and he kissed my lips. "You look sexy as hell by the way," he commented, as we headed out the club and to his car.

Mission accomplished, I thought.

JULIUS

One of the trap houses kept coming up short with my fucking money and I felt the need to drop by myself. Chico acted like he couldn't get the job done. Sometimes in life, things were done better when you did them your damn self.

"These niggas have pretty much signed their death certificate," I said as I headed over to the house with Tim in tow.

"Yeah, what did Chico say?" Tim asked frowning.

"He just said he didn't know who the fuck it was and for me to check it out," I responded shaking my head. What did I need his ass for if I was gone do this? I got Hugo on my back, all for a nigga who was slacking.

"Ain't that what you hired him for?" Tim questioned as if he was reading my mind.

"Yeah, but clearly he ain't a good fit," I said as we pulled up near the trap.

Tim and I hopped out the car and headed up the small walkway. When I walked in, everyone was sitting there chilling like they were on a damn vacation or something. Once they noticed me, they all jumped up. I was tempted to just blast the whole damn room with bullets.

"Why the fuck y'all parlaying when my fucking money is missing?" I boomed.

"Aye boss, we been trying-"

"Somebody about to die right fuckin now! Y'all got two options. Tell me who the culprit is, or I'm lighting every single one of you up," I spat. I was ready too. I had just enough bullets to kill every single one of these little niggas.

"It was Pat man," everyone spoke up simultaneously.

"Man look, I got a good reason. Moms was-" my worker Patrick tried to explain.

"Get the fuck up and let's go nigga," I yelled. Patrick jumped up and walked over by Tim and I.

"As for the rest of y'all, I'm gone drop by randomly and if I see y'all chilling again, I'm killing everyone," I said nonchalantly like it was nothing. In all actuality, it was nothing to me to kill each and every one of these niggas.

"Got it boss," they replied.

"Get yo' ass outside!" Tim yelled as he pushed Patrick outside the house.

As we walked down the walkway, a black Oldsmobile drove by slowly. The next thing I knew, an AK came out the back window and started filling the three of us up with bullets. I saw a bullet go straight through Patrick's head and knock him to the floor. I dropped down as well and pulled Tim with me.

"Hugo said die slow nigga!" the shooter yelled.

The car sped off, as my workers ran outside with their guns shooting at them. I heard one of them yell to call the ambulance, just before I blacked out. My last thoughts were of my beautiful wife and kids and how I left them here without me.

I woke up and saw I was in the hospital. I was thanking God that I was alive, even though I was in pain. I looked around the room and saw only Rashad, Dash, and Leese in the room. Where was my wife? I'm laid up in the hospital and she probably out clubbing again. I shook my head at the thought.

"Wh-Wh- Natalia," I said realizing my throat was too dry to talk in full sentences.

Rashad stood up and poured me some ice water to drink. He handed me the cup and I downed three more refills before feeling like I could speak.

"Where is Natalia?" I asked again but clearly.

"She just left," Rashad replied.

"Why did she leave?" I frowned.

"She was here all night and she needed to bathe and feed Jackson and Harmony," Rashad said as if I was tripping.

"Yeah right. She probably out being a fucking hoe," I spat and stared at the blank white wall.

"Bruh, she literally just left like thirty minutes ago. I'm sure the last thing on her mind is fucking another nigga," Dash chimed in. "She said she's coming back in an hour," he added.

"What, you fucking her now?" I scowled. Since when did he start wanting to defend Natalia? If he was fucking her, I would kill his ass without the slightest bit of hesitation.

"Nigga no, I just know she wouldn't do you like that," Dash frowned.

"Whatever. Fuck her," I replied and laid back down. "Where is Tim?" I asked as I suddenly remembered he was with me when I got shot.

"He uh, he didn't make it dawg," Leese shook his head as he stared at the floor.

"What? What the fuck you mean he didn't make it?" I felt myself getting emotional as I sat back up.

"The bullet went through his eye and entered his head," Rashad added. I just laid back down because I was speechless.

I tried to save him and didn't even succeed. I couldn't believe Tim was gone. Tim was like another brother to Rashad and I. I couldn't wait to get back at Hugo. I was mad that he shot me, but I was enraged that he killed my brother from another mother.

NATALIA

Now that my kids were fed, bathed and dressed, I could pass them off to Winnie. I knew she was here to do all that for me, but I enjoyed taking care of my own babies. I just needed her to watch them sometimes. I wouldn't have them growing up calling her mommy or crying when I took them away from her. That would definitely break my heart.

I threw on some black skinny jeans and an army green tube top, so I could head back out to the hospital. I couldn't believe someone had shot my baby. I prayed nonstop while he was in surgery and God came through for me. I smiled at the thought as I sped back to be by his side.

My phone buzzed as I was leaving, and I saw it was a text from Lucy. I rolled my eyes up in my head because she had no reason to be contacting me. Our friendship was over in my book. She had stabbed me in the back too many damn times. It was sad to think about because we used to be so close, but oh well, nothing lasts forever.

I walked down the hallway of the hospital, headed to Julius' room and ran right into Rashad coming out.

"Don't mind his attitude right now," Rashad commented and shook his head.

"What do you mean?" I asked, but Rashad just shook his head and walked away.

I walked into the room and saw Franceska sitting next to Julius, holding his hand. He was laying there staring at the ceiling, like he was in deep thought. I became just as angry as I was at the club that night. I couldn't keep allowing him to do me this way.

"Julius, why is she here?" I asked.

"Cause I'm his girl," she replied nastily.

"You're not his girl! He's married to me bitch!" I yelled and showed my ring finger in case she needed proof.

"Natalia, just go back to wherever you just were for the past hour," Julius said calmly.

"What?" I was so confused right now. I don't remember the doctor saying he had memory loss. I was with him the whole damn night. He couldn't be serious right now.

"Since you just now showing up, you can take your ass back home," he said clenching his jaw. "Or to whatever nigga's house you was at," he added.

"I was here all night with you! I left for one hour Julius, so that I could take care of *our* kids and at least shower and feed myself," I said feeling tears well up. Why was he always on some bullshit? We would be good and then he would always find a reason to trip out on me.

"Aight well, I got my girl here, so I don't need your services anymore," he replied and waved me off. He lifted Franceska's hand and kissed the back of it while looking me in the eyes. She smirked at me with a face that said, *yeah bitch, I won.*

"You want to be with her Julius?" I asked to make sure. I was tired of his games.

"He already is with me boo," she replied for him.

I nodded and slid my rings off my finger. I sat them on the table next to him and he looked at me with a surprised expression. I didn't say another word as I left the hospital room. Tears escaped my eyes in abundance, as I walked down to the car. I couldn't keep letting Julius treat me this way. Maybe it was better that we stay apart since it seemed we could never be happy.

3 WEEKS LATER

My little stunt I pulled in the hospital really pissed Natalia off. She was not fucking with me whatsoever. I sent flowers, jewelry, candy, clothes, everything I could think of, and she still wouldn't budge. When I showed up at the house, she would go sleep in the other room if I was in the bedroom. I was still smashing Franceska and she wasn't giving me any problems since she thought she was finally my girl. I shook my head at the thought. I knew I shouldn't have been fucking with anybody while trying to get my wife back at the same time, but shit happens.

I headed to my lawyer, Benjamin's house because he said he wanted to talk to me about something. I only spoke to him when I had some charges pending or something like that, so I wasn't sure why he felt the need to meet me. Everything I'd recently done was dancing around in my head, making me wonder if I'd been as careful as I'd thought.

I pulled up at his crib and pulled out my phone to text Natalia. I would text her all day, hoping that I would get a response one of these days. I was not giving up on her sexy ass, no matter what. I was kicking myself for pulling that bitch move at the hospital. If only a nigga could go back in time.

"So what's up Benny?" I smiled and sat down on his couch.

"I got something I think you want to know Julius," he said shaking his head and sitting down on the couch across from me.

"I'm listening," I replied shrugging.

"So, I have a friend who works at the lab and he let me know whose prints were on the drugs found in your car," he started to explain.

"Menzo?" I asked already knowing the answer.

"A Franceska Cruz," he replied.

Did this nigga really just tell me Franceska's ass set me up? Them fucking lab results couldn't possibly be right. I didn't want to believe that I was laid up with this bitch, and she was the one who threw me in jail. She was the reason I was away from my family? Nah, that shit couldn't have been right. It better not have been right for her sake.

"You sure Benny?" I frowned.

"I'm positive Julius. She was the last one to touch the drugs. If we put two and two together, it's obvious who put them in your vehicle that day," he said while giving me an assuring look. No wonder she disappeared for a while, after dropping me off at home the day I was released from jail.

"Thanks Benny," I said standing up to leave.

"Take care Julius," he said as I walked out of his crib.

I hopped in my G-Wagon and sped to this bitch's apartment. She was gone fucking die tonight. The thought of me dissing my wife for this bitch made me sick to my damn stomach. Especially when deep down, I didn't even want her ass. I was fucking up royally and too damn much.

"Hey daddy, I wish you would've told me you were coming through," Franceska said letting me in her crib.

"You set me up?" I asked getting straight to the point.

"What? Hell no. When?" she frowned in confusion. Damn she was a good actress. If I didn't have proof, I may have believed her.

"When you put those fucking drugs in my car bitch," I said through gritted teeth, while closing the gap between us.

"I-I didn't-"

PHEW!
PHEW!
PHEW!
I put my silencer on and shot her ass in the head. I hit up my cleanup crew to get rid of her ass, and wipe the place down. It seemed like all the hoes that I'd recruited in the past were somehow coming back to get me in the worst fucking way. This was all the more reason I needed to get back to the only woman I've ever loved and the only woman who has ever had my fucking back, regardless of how fucked up I did her. I needed my lady back and I was gonna get her. I didn't deserve her which is why I needed to do everything possible to keep her.

I was deciding on whether or not I should divorce Julius. I was sure about it after what he did in his hospital room that day, but he had really been trying to make up with me. I was proud of myself though, for being strong and not just letting him come back to me. It had been a long and lonely month without him, but I needed this time to think anyway.

Today I had some errands to run, so I wanted to get a head start. It was 10am already and I felt like I was running late, so I had Winnie dress my babies. I hated getting started on errands late because you never finished them when that happened.

"Good morning."

I turned around to see Julius walking into the bedroom. His cologne made me feel all warm inside and I knew I missed him. I wanted to run to him and give him a hug, but he didn't deserve that. It was crazy how a simple fragrance did so much to me.

"I'm about to leave," I replied. I didn't know why I said that.

"Sit down baby girl," he said closing the door behind him.

"I said I have to leave Julius," I repeated as he walked closer to me. My voice was starting to tremble, and I knew the tears were coming.

"Sit," he said again and sat me on the lounge chair in our room.

He kneeled down in front of me and reached in his pocket to pull out my wedding ring. He tried to slide it on my finger, but I snatched away. An evil smile appeared on his face, as he grabbed my hand back and slid it on successfully.

"I'm divorcing you," I said and wiped my falling tears.

"Baby," he started and exhaled heavily. "I'm sorry for what I said in the hospital room. I was angry that Tim died and that you weren't there when I woke up," he added.

"I was there the whole time Julius! I was only gone for an hour," I cried.

"I know baby. But like my mother said, men are like babies. We just need attention and shit all the time. When I woke up I wanted to see you there, and I got my little feelings hurt when you weren't," he said kissing the back of my hand.

"I didn't know you had feelings," I scoffed.

"Well I do, especially when it comes to you and my kids, ma. I know you love me but I was just being selfish with you. Sometimes I just want all your attention and when I feel I'm not getting it, I act out," he chuckled. "I hate to admit that, but it's true. You don't gotta worry about me being like that no more though. This month away from you made me realize I always have your attention and love baby girl," he added.

"You're my life Julius, I would never neglect you," I sniffled letting the tears fall.

"I know that. You never have. So, can we be husband and wife again?" he smiled and I got lost in his beautiful face. I nodded because I felt like I couldn't speak. "Thank God," he replied and leaned up to kiss my lips. I cupped his face and tongued him down, like I'd never see him again.

"I missed you," I whispered in between kisses.

"I missed you more baby," he replied.

"Now come on, I need to go to Target," I smiled standing up.

"You be using me," he chuckled.

"How so?" I smiled as I dusted off my skinny jeans.

"Cause you just want me to come so I can push the stroller and lift the heavy stuff," he laughed as he stood up.

"So," I laughed as well.

"Well, let's start with you," he chuckled and lifted me up bridal style, to carry me out.

Jackson, Harmony, Julius and I all spent the whole day together. It didn't even feel like I was running errands because I had missed us being a family so much. Julius was right though, it was a relief to not have to push the double stroller, or put all the grocery bags into the trunk. After all the errands, we went out to dinner and I was literally on cloud nine like I always was when we were together.

"Are you happy to be home?" I asked Julius as we laid in bed.

"Beyond," he exhaled.

"What about Franceska?" I asked.

"She won't be snooping around us no more," he replied. "But, you know what I miss more than you?" he smiled and started to kiss down my stomach.

"What?" I snickered.

"This," he responded kissing my vagina. "Mmmm," he moaned as he started to lick and suck slowly.

"Ahhh," I cooed and moved away some.

He got up and placed a pillow against the headboard. "Put your head against the headboard," he ordered.

I did as I was told, because I knew he always did that when he didn't want me pulling away. Once my head was against the pillow and I had nowhere to move, he dipped his head back between my legs and took me to the high heavens.

JULIUS

Now that I had my family back, it was time to get this nigga Hugo. I was gonna kill his ass for sure, but before that, I wanted him to suffer. I wanted him to suffer mentally, physically and most importantly, financially. Nothing hurt a nigga more than messing with his money. A man was more scared of losing his coins than getting killed. By saying that, it was time to pack up my family and take a trip to Indiana.

Natalia tried to protest coming with me, but there was no way I was leaving her behind again. I learned my lesson when that nigga Greg kidnapped her. I was not about to take that damn risk again. We just got back together and I didn't want anything pulling us apart, especially not with Hugo on the prowl, because he was a sick ass nigga.

I was originally gonna stay at my old home, but I knew that wasn't a good idea. Every fucking body knew where I lived and with a price on my head from the current king of the city, it wasn't safe to harbor my family there. I rented out a nice little four-bedroom condo in Noblesville, Indiana, which is about forty-five to fifty minutes north of Indianapolis. I needed my family and Winnie as far away as possible, from this war that was about to occur.

"Aight baby girl, I'm about to head to Indianapolis and I will be back tonight," I told Natalia as she laid in bed with Jackson and Harmony.

"Tonight at what time?" she asked.

"Like 11pm," I replied leaning in the doorway.

"Okay," she said standing up and laying Harmony on her stomach.

"Don't go anywhere today please," I said.

"I won't, I don't know my way around this city," she smiled.

"Right," I chuckled and went over to kiss her lips. "Call me if you need me and I will check up on you periodically throughout the day," I added as I kissed my kids' cheeks.

"Alright," she exhaled heavily.

I sped over to Rashad's condo, which was in Noblesville as well, because he and our team needed to put together a plan. Shit was about to get real and we had no time for mistakes or unplanned strategies. This was not a time to be caught slipping.

"Sup," Rashad said as he opened his front door.

"What's up with you? You good?" I frowned.

"Yeah, Paula just tripping," he said putting on his shoes.

"These girls be driving us crazy, don't they?" I smirked.

"Right, she's mad cause I didn't bring her with me," he shook his head.

"Why didn't you?" I asked.

"I don't know, I ain't really feeling her at the moment. She's been bugging me constantly. You know I ain't ever been into bitches who nag," he said as he walked out the front door.

I just shrugged my shoulders because Paula wasn't even a factor to me. Unless she was finna help with taking down Hugo, I didn't give a damn.

"Aight, so Bart has agreed to ship to us here in Indianapolis so that we can start selling on Hugo's turf," I started.

"Who's watching everything back in Charleston?" Dash asked.

"I got Jabari and Luke on that. Plus, we only gone be here three weeks' tops, so ain't too much they have to do. The shipments are already set to get there from Antonio. All they have to do is pick it up and get the product exchanged with the list of people I gave them. By the time a new shipment comes, we will be back," I replied.

"You think we gone get Hugo that quick?" Leese frowned.

"I know we will," I smiled. "Now first thing's first. We gone hit up a nice amount of his workers and shit, and let that nigga know we're here. Once we do that, we're gonna start pushing weight on his blocks. Any other niggas of his that come up, we just gone blast them off too," I said.

"So we're planning to take them out two nights from today," Rashad added and I nodded.

"Dash, you and Alonzo are gonna pick up the shipment from Bart and get it to our niggas to push," I said and they nodded and smiled.

"I know I'm going with y'all, right?" Leese smiled.

"That's right," I smiled back.

I leaned back in my chair and smiled at the room full of my team. Hugo was gonna regret ever fucking with a nigga like me. I'd be sure to send flowers to his widow though.

NATALIA

I was relaxing in the bedroom and constantly glancing at the clock next to the bed. It was 11:10pm and I hoped Julius was coming home soon like he said. I knew what was going on, because I had been reading his text messages and I was scared for his life. Hugo almost killed him back in Charleston, and I didn't want that to happen again. Not that I didn't think Ju could handle himself, because I knew he could, but I just didn't want him getting hurt. We needed him to grow old with us.

My phone buzzed, letting me know I had a text message, and I quickly grabbed it hoping it was my husband checking in with me.

Marlon: I wanna see you.

Me: Hell no nigga.

I frowned at my phone as if he could see me.

Marlon: Come on, I miss you. Lucy and I are over.

Me: It's not about Lucy. I just don't want you.

Marlon: Let me just apologize, face to face.

Me: No! I'm not even in Charleston anyway.

Marlon: I know. I'm in Indiana at the moment too.

I frowned up and locked my phone. Was he following me? He couldn't have been following me. I hoped he wasn't because that would mean I ended up with another crazy nigga. How did he even know I was here? What about me attracted these crazy ass dudes? First it was Frank, and now possibly Marlon. I was not trying to get kidnapped again.

Just then, I heard the front door open. I climbed out the bed and lightly jogged to stand at the top of the stairs. I saw Julius and I ran down to him fast as hell. As soon as I reached him, he picked me up in his arms.

"What's wrong with you?" he quizzed.

"I was worried," I smiled back.

"No need to do that baby," he said as he carried me upstairs to our bedroom. "I need to shower," he added putting me down and exhaling heavily. "What are you doing?" he cheesed when he saw me following him.

"I wanna come too," I chuckled.

He grinned, then closed the door and kissed me. We undressed and then stepped into the nice hot shower. He stood under the showerhead and closed his eyes, as the water covered his muscular body. I watched in awe at how perfect he was. He opened his eyes, smiled at me and then pulled me close to him. He moved from under the head and put me under it so that I could get wet too.

"You're so beautiful," he said running a finger down my wet body. He then joined me under the showerhead for a passionate kiss.

I was wondering if I should mention the fact that Marlon had followed us to Indiana. I decided not to, since Julius already had enough on his plate. He didn't need to worry about Marlon and his unrequited love for me; that was small potatoes.

JULIUS

Tonight was the night that we would spray all Hugo's blocks with heat. This was so much easier, because I knew all his spots. I used to work for the nigga, so all of this shit was a piece of cake. I wanted to make sure he regretted fucking with me and paid for killing Tim. Unfortunately, the niggas he had working for him had to be eliminated because of their boss' dirt.

"Y'all ready?" I asked Leese and Rashad.

"You know I am," Leese replied and Rashad nodded.

We got into the unmarked car we'd obtained and made sure everything was loaded up. Rashad was doing the driving and Leese and I would be shooting. We decided to go in order of distance, to make sure we didn't miss any areas. I felt bad that these innocent people had to die, but those feelings would quickly dissipate whenever I thought about the fact that Tim was no longer with us.

"Should we rob the traps?" Leese asked chuckling.

"What y'all think?" I smirked.

"Shit, might as well get that nigga's cash too," Rashad shrugged.

"I don't know if we will have time to rob and get to everybody, before word gets out and they start calling that nigga," I replied trying to think. "I also don't want to give his little niggas a chance to shoot," I said still thinking.

"Fuck it, let's just do it," Rashad smiled.

"Nigga, I have a wife and kids. Nothing is just fuck it for me anymore," I chuckled.

"These niggas ain't no match for us Ju," Leese said with a pleading tone. His crazy ass was always trying to do the most. I fucked with him though, because he was down to do whatever.

"I can't stand y'all reckless asses, but let's go," I chuckled.

"Hell yeah, nigga!" Rashad beamed and cranked up the whip.

We got to the first trap and it was dead just like I knew it would be. It was at that period where it was too late in the night, yet too early. I knew these traps like the back of my damn hand. We all exited the car after making sure Rashad now had a gun with him. We weren't wearing masks either, because I wanted this nigga to know who fucked his shit up in case there were any bystanders witnessing this massacre. Already knowing where the money was, we walked in and just emptied two shots each into the three niggas that were sitting there. While Rashad and I took the money out of the walls, Leese spread gasoline around the whole house. Once we got all the money, Leese lit a match and threw it into the place. It immediately became engulfed in flames as we sped off to repeat our steps.

"Aye man, don't shoot. I'll give y'all what y'all want," one of the guys at the next house begged with his hands up. We'd already blew the other worker's head open.

PHEW!

PHEW!

Rashad pumped two in his dome and we slid over the bookshelves to retrieve the money behind it. These traps were making a cool amount of money, but nowhere near what my shit was bringing in back home in Charleston.

"Should we take the product?" Leese asked as he started his gasoline routine.

"Nah, this shit is weak as hell," I said shaking my head and throwing the bag over my shoulder.

"Aye, what the fuck!" someone yelled and let off a shot into Rashad's shoulder.

I immediately turned around and shot the nigga in the head. I assumed he was a worker that wasn't around during our arrival. I grabbed the bag from Rashad and helped him out the house, as Leese drug the new guy in, and lit the match.

"Should we take him to the hospital?" Leese asked as Rashad held onto his shoulder.

"Nah, it was just a graze," Rashad replied inspecting it.

"You sure nigga?" I frowned.

"Yeah muthafucka, I know what a graze is," he laughed.

I shrugged my shoulders as he continued to drive the car. I hoped it was only a graze because people always try to underestimate a simple shoulder shot. That shit killed Selena, so I knew it could be fatal. We continued our route and successfully killed, robbed and torched the rest of the trap houses Hugo had.

"I don't even want this nigga's money," I smiled.

"What we gone do with it?" Leese asked.

I looked out the window as we drove and saw a homeless man with a sign. "Pull over Shad," I said to my brother.

"Why nigga?" he frowned.

"Nigga, just pull over," I spat shaking my head.

He did as I asked and I reached in the back for a duffle bag of money. I grabbed a plastic bag to put the majority of the money in and then got out the car. I didn't want someone from Hugo's camp to recognize the bag and accuse the homeless man of having something to do with the robberies, which is why I changed it. Once I was out, I started to walk towards the homeless man. He started to back up a little; I guess he was scared that I was about to harm him.

"Here you go man," I said handing him the plastic bag.

He hesitated but then took the bag from me. His wife and two daughters emerged from the alley, to see what was going on. It broke my heart to see him out here starving with his family. I knew when a man couldn't provide, it killed his pride. That's why my mother's boyfriend hit her all the time. He didn't have money and every time he couldn't put food in our mouths, he went upside her head to release his anger. When I was twelve, I saved up any money I had at the time, bought some poison for this nigga's food and killed him silently. Everyone thought he'd just had a heart attack. I thought we would be good after that, but my mom got a new man and he got her hooked on dope. Our relationship became next to nothing once that pipe became her priority. I'd been providing for myself ever since.

"Thank you so much sir. God bless you," the homeless man said snapping me out of my thoughts. I nodded and jogged back to the car.

For the rest of the night, we gave the money to homeless people that we knew for sure weren't drug addicts. I'd worked the streets long enough to recognize the regulars around here. All night I wondered what I would do if I couldn't provide for my family. That would never happen though, because I invested my shit. This drug game could only last for so long. If you weren't smart with your money, you would end up with a lot of hard work completed but nothing to show for it. Hugo was about to be the perfect example.

"You need to let my wife at least look at it," I said to my brother, after dropping Leese off at his condo in Noblesville.

"If that'll ease yo' little bitch ass mind, then I will," he joked.

"Fuck you," I laughed as we pulled into my driveway.

When we walked into the house, I smelled freshly cooked food. It was 4am, so I wasn't sure why the food smelled like it was just done. I walked into the kitchen and saw Natalia sitting at the table, sleep. She had on a short pajama gown, showing her sexy legs and her long thick hair in one single braid.

"Why you not in the bed, ma?" I asked, shaking her lightly.

"Oh, I wanted to give you your food," she half smiled, with her eyes low.

"Ma, you ain't have to do that," I chuckled and sat at the table.

"Yes I did. You didn't eat breakfast today," she said, standing up to walk over to the oven.

"Smells good in here," Rashad commented as he walked in.

"Why are you bleeding?" Natalia asked with her eyes bucked.

"Oh, I'm good ma. Just a little graze," Rashad smiled.

Natalia shook her head and then made us both a plate of chicken and cheese, angel hair pasta. After we scarfed it down, she doctored up Rashad's shoulder. Thank God he was right about it only being a graze.

For the rest of night, I tossed and turned because my thoughts wouldn't let me sleep. I was thinking about if Hugo had caught wind of what we just did. I hoped he did because I couldn't wait to get a reaction out of him. Somehow, my mind also drifted to Bianca. I wondered if they released her ass from jail yet. I was gonna make some calls to my boys in Charleston, to see if she was out in the streets.

BIANCA EVANS

Today was the greatest day of my life. I was getting released from jail after only being in here for ten months. I got eighteen months at my sentencing, but I was released early for good behavior. I had to go through all these psych evaluations to make sure that I wasn't crazy, and I passed with flying colors. I wasn't fucking crazy; I was just in love with a man who never loved me. It made me sick to even speak those words, but it was true.

See, it all became so complicated. I didn't think my lie through to the end. I was too busy living in the moment to plan a plausible outcome. I needed to present a baby to Julius and I thought, why not just get the one that I've been using this whole time. I went to visit Lizzie, you know, the girl who was helping me. Once she left the room to go use the restroom, I snatched up her son and booked out to my car. I was halfway to my apartment by the time she realized what I'd done and started blowing up my phone. I texted Julius that he could come see our baby and then shut my phone off so she would stop bothering me. We weren't even together for a good five minutes, before that bitch had the police busting into my apartment to arrest Ju and I. Funny enough, the only thing I could think about while being arrested, was if Julius would ever forgive me. Isn't that crazy? Not once was I worried about being in jail or my record being trashed. All I was worried about was Julius. Julius, Julius, Julius; he had completely taken over my life.

However, my days of running behind Julius were over. I still loved him, but my time in jail made me realize he's not worth the good love I have to give. I gave that man everything and for what? For him to run off into the sunset with another woman. That shit hurt like no other pain in the world. As a wise woman once said, you can teach a dog how to walk and he'll walk off with another bitch. That's just what Julius did, too. I'll tell you one thing that would make more money than anything in the world, would be a cure to a broken heart. I would've paid top dollar for someone to stitch my shit up, because it was in complete shambles.

"Ready to go?" the correctional officer asked me after I collected my belongings.

"Yes, I am," I replied smiling.

I walked out to see if my ride was here and it was. A smile crept across my face as I switched over to the all-black Cadillac Escalade. I tugged on the handle and climbed into the backseat smiling.

"Welcome home," Hugo smiled.

Yeah, Hugo. This nigga flew all the way to Charleston to pick me up from jail. We'd pretty much been talking to one another the whole time I was here. He was telling me he had some beef with Julius, outside of the connect. Now he was saying he had some more shit with him and he wanted him dead. As bad as Julius hurt me, I was willing to help anyone who would hurt him as well.

"It feels good," I smiled. "So what's the plan?" I asked as the driver pulled off.

"So are you really over Julius?" he asked puffing on his cigar. *Why does it matter?* I thought to myself.

"Beyond, I just wanna get back at him for doing me so dirty," I responded coldly.

"You're sexy as hell," Hugo winked.

Hugo was an okay looking man, but way too old for me. He was about forty-seven years old, but in pretty good shape. He was light-skinned, bald and buff as fuck. I knew he had a wife who was dumb as hell, thinking her husband was faithful to her. They had five kids together and she spent her days caring for them. That sounded so boring to me; sitting at home being a damn babysitter, until my cheating ass husband gets home. Yeah right. A part of me felt bad for her stupid ass.

"Thanks Hugo," I said dryly. "So what are we gonna do?" I quizzed.

"Well, you know his girl very well, so I think we should go for the gusto," he snickered and licked his lips. Hugo was such a pervert.

"Kill her?" I asked to make sure.

"Eventually, but I want to kidnap her. Get me a couple strokes of that pussy and then maybe get some money to give her back. Shit, she may not wanna go back," he replied running his tongue across his teeth.

What was it about Natalia? She was pretty but damn, she seemed to be some rare dish that everyone wanted to try. I hated that little bitch.

"So you need me to go get her? I don't even know where they live out here in Charleston," I complained.

"That bitch ass nigga is back there in Indiana and I know he didn't leave his little sexy wife at home," he replied. "Bitch ass nigga burned down all my traps," he said damn near balling his face up in a knot.

"Oh shit Hugo!" I yelped covering my mouth.

"Yeah, that nigga has done too much shit to me. Stole my connect, killed my nephew, took one of my best workers and now he's fucking up my revolving income," he said lighting up another cigar.

"I didn't know Ju was doing you so dirty," I said shaking my head. "Who is your nephew?" I asked. The thought of Julius out here thuggin' made my panties super wet. He was always crazy as fuck, but this was a little bit more. I don't think I would ever be over his ass, which is why he needed to be six feet under.

"Young man named Frank. I promised my sister I would kill Julius and I will," he said taking a puff. "I sent his brother Marlon to do it, but he ended up falling for the nigga's wife," he added shaking his head.

"You still got money to pay me right?" I frowned.

"Bitch, I ain't broke! I just ain't got no money coming in!" he boomed. I let it slide because I knew he was just frustrated that his pockets would be temporarily dry.

"Just set up some new areas," I shrugged. *This drug shit couldn't be that hard,* I thought.

"The nigga done took over my blocks. He out here selling way better shit. I can't even find who is working for him to kill they ass. But all I know is, ain't nobody buying from the little niggas I do have left," he said running his hand over his face.

"Damn," was all I could say. I really ain't care about what he was bitching about.

I wasn't here to console him; I was here to take down the nigga that fucked me over. Hugo and I had a mutual hate and all I wanted to talk about was taking care of that.

"Well, Natalia is always watching the kids, so I'm sure we can catch her at Julius' crib, run in there and snatch her," I smiled.

"Aight, you know that house well. So give my boys the ins and outs of it so we can get her. My dick is hard already at the thought of pounding that sweet young bitch," he said biting his lip and looking straight ahead. *Pervert*, I thought.

"Yep," I simply replied.

"But first I wanna try you," he bit his lip and released his short fat dick.

"Hugo, that was not a part of the deal, I'm not fucking you," I spat, glancing back and forth between the driver and Hugo.

He grabbed my neck and squeezed as tight as he could. He twisted up his face and then clenched his teeth before speaking.

"You'll do whatever the fuck I tell your pretty ass to do," he whispered through clenched teeth. "Take your fucking jeans off," he added and threw me backwards.

I was about to speak up, until an AK emerged from the row of seats behind us. I looked at the shooter, who was frowning and ready to blow my head open. A tear slipped out of my eye, as I slowly began to remove my jeans and underwear. Before I could get them off good,

Hugo tugged me over onto his lap. He sucked and licked on my neck, as he opened the condom wrapper and slid it down on his dick. Once it was on, he slammed me down onto his rod.

"Ahh!" I screamed out at the pain.

Hugo gripped tightly onto my waist and humped upward like a jackrabbit. I was barely wet, as he thrust into me as if his life depended on it. He threw his head back and started to shiver a little while, biting his lip.

"Yeah, take this dick," he groaned. *What dick?* I thought.

He sped up even faster and I looked in the back to see his shooter laughing to himself. I would've much rather fucked him than Hugo's disgusting ass.

"Arrrgghhhh!" Hugo growled as if he were a bear in the forest. "Fuck!" he yelled, gyrating violently as if he were having a seizure.

I quickly climbed off him and slipped my panties back onto my dry pussy. Hugo sat there panting with his head thrown back and eyes closed. His small dick was still inside the condom, as he lay there like an old ass grandpa.

"No wonder Julius wifed you for a little bit," he smirked as he looked over at me.

I turned my lip up, folded my arms over my chest and rolled my eyes. I stared out the window thinking about how Julius continued to ruin my life, when all I ever gave him was love. Here I was having to sacrifice my body to a nasty ass old man because of him. Julius was gonna go down and I didn't care how I had to go about doing it.

NATALIA

I was so bored being out here in Noblesville. I wished so badly that we could've at least stayed in Indianapolis so I could do some stuff. I knew being here was for my safety but still, I missed going out to eat with Paula, or taking my babies to the park. Julius promised that we would be gone in one week, and I couldn't wait.

Being the wonderful husband that he is, he agreed to get some board games for Winnie and I, before he headed out to Indianapolis. We'd been playing Monopoly all morning, but now I was tired and hungry. While Winnie got up to make lunch for the babies and me, I decided to play with Jackson. My phone rang, while I was kissing his fat cheeks and I saw it was Lucy. I missed her, but I refused to admit that and be friends again.

"Hello?" I answered.

"How are you?" she asked.

"I'm fine. What do you want?" I frowned as if she could see me.

"I miss you Natalia! This is dumb. I told you I didn't know that you and Marlon were dating. I thought you and Julius were good," she replied pleading.

"We were good. I just... I don't know," I exhaled.

"I promise I wouldn't do that. I know that whole thing with Julius in Vegas was not a good look, but I was going through it then. Now I'm good. I'm the old Lucy," she said and I could hear her smiling.

"The Lucy that had my back?" I asked.

"Yes Natalia. I never stopped loving you. Even when I was on my jealous tip," she chuckled.

"So what's been going on?" I inquired, happy that she'd called me.

"Well, I've been in cosmetology school because I want to do hair. Lumar is such a good baby," she said. I really missed Lucy.

"Any prospects?" I smiled.

"No, I'm working on being by myself for now. For as long as I can remember, I've always had some type of nigga. I need a break," she huffed.

"Yeah," I said cheesing at Jackson and rubbing Harmony's back as she slept.

"So Mrs. Tate, what have you been up to?" she questioned.

"Back in Indiana right now. But before I left, Julius said he would help me open a cupcake bakery," I beamed at the thought.

"That is such a good idea Nat. Your cupcakes are so good. I remember you used to make cupcakes for us every Saturday. Remember that?" she giggled.

"Yeah I do," I laughed. "I missed you Lucy," I finally said.

"I missed you too," she replied. "When do you come back?" she quizzed.

"Next week, maybe we can get the babies together," I offered.

"I can't wait," she said.

"Okay, talk to you later," I smiled feeling all giddy inside. I loved my best friend and I couldn't wait to spend more time with her.

After about an hour, Winnie had enchiladas and baked beans ready. I was starved and ready to eat like I was in jail. Once I ate and made sure Jackson and Harmony ate, I bathed them and put them to bed. I was lying in the upstairs bedroom, scrolling on Instagram, when a text from Paula came through.

Paula: *Is Rashad near you?*

Me: *No, why?*

Paula: *That nigga is pissing me off!*

Me: Why?

I was surprised because I thought she and Rashad were good. He seemed so happy and relaxed out here, so you would never know he was having problems with her. Rashad usually wore his emotions on the outside, so you would know if he was bothered.

Paula: He barely answers my fucking calls and texts. But the worst part is, that he didn't bring me with him. Ju brought you!

Me: To keep me safe Paula, I'm sure he didn't mean anything by it.

Paula: So fuck me? I shouldn't need to be safe?

Me: Not that, but nobody really knows you as Rashad's girlfriend. So it's unlikely that someone would come for you.

Paula: Oh and everybody knows about you and Julius? Lol

Me: Everyone knows I'm his wife.

Paula: Everybody except him. Goodnight.

I wasn't trying to be mean to Paula, I was trying to make her feel better. I didn't want her to think that Rashad didn't bring her because he didn't care. I wanted her to think that he didn't bring her because he felt she was safe where she was. I guess it backfired, because she was taking the Lucy approach by insulting my relationship. Those comments didn't hurt anymore, because I knew Julius had changed. I didn't care about the past any longer. Julius had matured and I knew he was being faithful to me like he promised. He hadn't hit me since the day he promised he wouldn't either, so I had no reason to doubt him.

A part of me was curious to know why Rashad was dissing Paula. If she wouldn't have gotten mad with me just now, I would've asked her for more details. I've never known Paula to be the jealous or crazy type, so I was sure that whatever was going on was Rashad's fault.

LUCY OUISTIN

I decided to surprise Natalia in Indiana, so I booked a mid-week flight since it was the cheapest. I was so happy that she agreed to make up after that whole Marlon thing, because I felt like I was dying without her. We became so attached to each other over the years, and I needed her. I honestly thought she and Marlon's relationship didn't go past the night at IHOP. I mean, she hadn't talked to me in forever, so how was I supposed to know what was going on in her life? Whatever. All I knew is that I missed my best friend and that I wanted to be like we were before.

As far as Marlon, I stopped fucking with him after Natalia caught us together. He tried to pretend like he was so into me, but I realized that shit was a lie. The way he left me naked in his bed to go chase after Natalia, showed me that his feelings for me weren't there or weren't as strong as the ones he had for Natalia. After him, I told myself I needed a break from guys. I just needed to focus on my career and raising my son. If a good man came along, then so be it, but my looking days were over. They'd brought me nothing but trouble, heartbreak and humiliation.

"This is the house," I said to the taxi driver so that he'd pull over.

"That'll be twenty-nine dollars and forty-four cents," he said giving me the total. I handed him $35, and got out of the car with my small suitcase.

I walked up the walkway and knocked lightly on the screen door. No one came to answer, so I had to end my surprise. I pulled out my cell phone and pressed Natalia's name so she could come to the door for me.

"Hey Lucy!" she answered.

"Hey, are you home?" I asked smiling.

"Yeah, I'm always *out here*," she exhaled.

"Okay. Come to the door, I'm outside," I grinned and fixed my shirt.

"What? Why?" she asked.

"Cause I'm in Indiana hoe!" I laughed. "I'm outside your house," I added.

"I don't see you," she said.

"I'm right at-" before I could finish, a black sack was placed over my head. "Ahhh! What!" I yelled and squirmed as I tried to get the bag off my head.

I heard Natalia yelling my name, as my phone slipped from my grasp. I was being dragged backwards as I fought wildly to either get the sack off my head or get away altogether. I was shouting to let me go, which came out low and muffled. I felt myself being put into a car and the car started to move, making me scream harder and louder. All of a sudden, the sack was snatched off and I didn't recognize any of these men. They all appeared to be about twenty-five or younger and had on all black.

"Where are you-"

Before I could finish, the guy sitting next to me placed a cloth over my mouth and nose. I fought violently, as he pressed my head against the glass while laughing. I felt myself getting weak, until I finally passed out.

"Who the fuck is this?!" I heard a deep voice yell.

"The girl, boss," someone replied.

My eyes fluttered and I kept blinking hoping to clear my vision up. I saw a big, buff, bald, light-skinned guy yelling at one of the guys that were in the car with me earlier.

"Did you go to the right house? This is not Natalia!" the buff guy yelled. *Natalia? Why were they trying to kidnap Natalia?* I wondered.

"Yes boss, I went to this address here!" he replied pointing to a crumpled up piece of paper.

"This is fucked up. This all fucked up," the buff guy yelled as he paced the room.

Suddenly, he pulled a gun from his waist and shot the guy in the head. I jumped and screamed, making him look at me. I tried to move away, but realized I was tied up. An evil grin appeared on his face as he walked over to me.

"You're just as beautiful though," he said kneeling in front of me. I turned my face away from him, as a tear slid down my face. "Who are you? You must know Natalia and Julius," he quizzed.

"No I don't," I said shaking my head.

"Don't fucking lie!" he yelled banging on a piece of the chair between my legs.

"Sh-she's my best friend," I stuttered.

"Well then you can help me get her," he smiled.

"No," I replied frowning.

"Either you help me get her, or I'm gone make you," he said standing to his feet.

"I said no," I replied in calm tone, while looking up at him.

WHAM!

He slapped the shit out of me and it hurt so badly. I'm surprised my neck didn't snap, due to his strength. However, I couldn't give Natalia up. I'd done too much to her already, I'd be damned if I got her killed or whatever he wanted to do with her. After a couple seconds of silence, he started to unbuckle his pants and my eyes got big.

"If you don't want this big dick shoved up that little pretty pussy of yours, you better tell me where your friend is," he said stroking his penis. It wasn't big, so maybe he was referring to another dick.

As much as I didn't want him to touch me, I couldn't give up. I didn't say anything as more tears flowed down my face. He nodded and started to untie me from the chair. He grabbed my arm roughly and tugged me over to his desk. He bent me over it, and ripped my panties off from under my skirt, as I screamed and squirmed.

"I have an STD," I lied hoping it worked.

"It's cool," he panted as he pushed my face into his hard wood desk.

I heard him rip open a condom and spit the package pieces onto the floor. After rolling it down, he rammed into my dry vagina.

"Ahhh!" I screamed.

"Fuck," he moaned as he pumped into me hard and fast.

I should've stayed my ass in Charleston. Thank God I didn't bring Lumar.

After having his way with me for about four dreadful minutes, he took me to a room and tied me back to a chair. This time he tied my ankles to the chair legs, making it impossible for me to move anything but my neck.

"Now, since you don't want to help, you can stay here until we find Natalia. Unless you grow the fuck up and help!" he screamed.

Even if I did want to give her up, I had no idea where she was. I thought she was at Julius' house in Indianapolis, just like they did. As he turned to walk out of the room, I prayed that he didn't find her and hurt her. She'd been through too much in life and deserved to be happy.

THAT NIGHT...

After I got the text from Hugo's boy Gee that Natalia had been kidnapped, I decided it was time to celebrate. I went and bought me some champagne because this would be the first day of my wonderful life. Since Julius broke my heart, Hugo was gonna break his by raping and killing his little hoe of a wife. I almost wished I could be there to watch. She deserved everything that was coming to her, since she wanted to steal people's man.

I was laid in the bed in my hotel room, just thinking about my life. I didn't want to stay here in Indiana because it brought back too many memories. My apartment in Charleston was no longer available since I went to jail. Plus, I didn't want to be in the same state as Julius anymore. I hated even saying his name because it hurt too much. We'd been broken up for almost three years now, and it still hurt to say his name. I shook my head at my thoughts. *Maybe I'd move to Florida and make a name for myself at KOD,* I thought as I reached for my champagne flute.

As I brought the glass up to my lips, I heard someone knocking at my hotel room door. I wasn't expecting anyone and Hugo had already paid me for the info on Natalia's whereabouts, so I was confused.

"Yes?" I yelled from behind the door.

"Housekeeping!" I heard a female voice say. *Housekeeping, at nine at night?* I wondered.

"Umm, why so late?" I shouted as I peered through the peephole at her.

"Forgot to put towels in the room Miss," she replied.

I swung open the door. "Okay, but please hurry-"

I was rushed by two masked men, sacked, and pulled out the back entrance of the hotel, screaming and kicking. The maid followed and hopped into the driver's seat. I was so scared because I knew Julius ordered this kidnapping. *Lord, please don't let me die tonight,* I pleaded in my head. I would do anything he wanted me to do in order to save my life.

After riding in the car for about thirty minutes, the car finally came to a stop. I was roughly grabbed out of the car and pulled in the left direction. They slammed me down into a chair and started to tie me to it.

"Julius! I'm sorry!" I screamed through the sack over my head. "I can help you get her back babe, please!" I cried

"Shut up bitch," I heard Hugo boom. *Hugo? What the fuck?* I thought. I was so confused.

Suddenly, the sack was snatched off my head and Hugo was standing right in front of me. The chick pretending to be a maid and the guy that sacked me left the room. If I wasn't baffled before, I was damn sure baffled as fuck now.

"Hugo, what are you doing?" I frowned.

"We got the wrong bitch!" he yelled as he glared down at me.

"Okay? How is that my fault? Untie me!" I shouted and squirmed as much as I could.

"Because you supplied the information. You told us Natalia would be at Julius' house," he scowled.

"Look, just give me more time. I can get you Natalia," I pleaded looking up at him.

"Nah, because now I don't trust you. You were apologizing to Julius a couple minutes ago," he said releasing his dick. "You was about to turn on me with your disloyal ass," he glared down at me.

"What are you-"

I shut my eyes and mouth, as Hugo released his urine all over my face and clothes. I couldn't believe this was happening to me. I hated Natalia even more now. Why was she so difficult? Natalia and Julius continued to cause all the bad things that happened in my life. I was so happy and carefree until she came into Julius' and my life. I'd been miserable and plagued with bad luck ever since!

"Such a sexy girl. What a waste," Hugo commented as he pulled his gun from his waist.

"Hugo ple-"

POW!

I endured all this for Julius' love. But as Jhene Aiko once sang, "Where I'm from, we live for the love, die for the love."

JULIUS

I drove to my old house just to see if anything had been out of order. I wanted to see if there were any signs that Hugo had tried to get at my family or me. When I pulled up, there was a pink suitcase in the walkway. It was open and had been ransacked and sifted through. *A bum must've seen and done this,* I thought. I recognized one of the dresses in the suitcase and racked my brain trying to remember who I saw it on. I looked to my right and saw an iPhone face down in the dirt. *I know that bum would be mad he missed this,* I laughed to myself. When I picked it up, I saw multiple calls and texts from Natalia. She was stored as Natalia Bff. *Lucy!* I said to myself. She wore that dress in Vegas to the Michael Jackson show. I grabbed her suitcase, ran to my car and sped to the meeting area we'd acquired. I called my people on the way there to let them know it was an emergency. Please God don't let this girl be dead.

"Nigga, what's going on?" Rashad asked with a concerned expression.

"That nigga Hugo got Lucy. I bet he was intending to get Natalia," I said trying to think of a plan.

"Fuck. You think he hurt her?" Dash asked.

"I'm sure he did. He's a pervert when it's females. Shit!" I yelled on the last part.

"Calm down bro," Rashad commented.

"Aight, look. If he still has her alive, it's only one place he's holding her, at his warehouse," I said.

"Well let's go!" Dash said.

"Nah, we gone go tonight," I replied.

"Nigga what? Why?" Leese frowned.

"Because Hugo ain't gone be there, it's too early. He goes to check on his hostages every night around 11:30pm," I said letting a smile creep across my face.

"Okay, but ain't that the opposite? Don't we want him not to be there?" Leese asked out of confusion.

"Nah, we gone kill two birds with one stone. We gone rescue Lucy and kill Hugo in the process," I nodded. "This is the plan. Rashad, you're gonna rescue Lucy. I'm gonna show up to distract the nigga since I'm who he wants. Once I say what I gotta say, I'm gone blast his ass. Once it's finished, Leese, you torch the warehouse. Dash, you stand guard and kill any nigga that shows up. I don't care who it is," I finished and everyone smiled.

"Sounds perfect," Dash smiled.

"Everybody meet here at 10pm. I want to have time to get there and time to stake the place out," I said.

"Got it. Since it's only 4pm right now, we can go to Noblesville and chill right?" Rashad asked.

"Yeah, that's actually best. That way we won't get caught slipping out here in Indianapolis," I replied standing.

"Aight bet," Rashad nodded.

Hugo had it coming. Boy did this nigga have it coming. Never fuck with a nigga who knows you and your businesses. And if you do, change shit up. This nigga hadn't switched out or changed one thing since I'd worked for him. I know because his traps were the same, his shipments were the same, even his lunchtime was the same. I had completely fucked his operation up. I intercepted his shipments, torched his trap houses, robbed his condo safes; I mean, he was hurting for sure. I should've killed him a little bit ago, but I wanted him to suffer mentally and financially first. Unfortunately, during that process, he kidnapped Lucy. She better not be dead though, or I was gonna come for that little wife of his.

NATALIA

Ever since my phone call with Lucy, I'd been biting my nails. Julius stayed in Indianapolis last night, so I hadn't seen him to say anything. I asked him to call me but he didn't. I was so upset with him I could choke him. Just as the thought crossed my mind, he walked through the door. It was about 5:30pm and he had the nerve to smile at me.

"Hey gorgeous," he said walking up to me.

"Don't talk to me," I pouted.

"I wasn't, I was talking to Harmony," he joked and smiled as he picked her up. He walked up the stairs to put her in bed for a nap, and I followed him.

"Where were you last night?" I yelled after we both left Harmony's room and entered ours.

"I was too tired to drive," he said as he started to undress.

"I texted you, telling you to call me."

"I know ma, and I was going to, but something happened," he exhaled and sat on the edge of the bed.

"Yeah, I think something is wrong with Lucy," I whined.

"Don't worry about it. She'll be good by tonight," he said.

"By tonight? What is the problem?" I asked folding my arms over my chest.

"Look babe, you don't need to-"

"What is wrong with Lucy?" I hollered cutting him off. I didn't have time for his bullshit.

"Hugo kidnapped her ma-"

"Oh my gosh!"

"But I'm gone get her tonight babe don't wor-"

"Tonight? Why not now? Go now Julius!" I cried.

"No Natalia, I have a plan in place. Just relax," he said frowning.

"Julius, if something happens to Lucy, I will never forgive you," I said breathing heavily. I didn't know what I was saying; I was just worried. Plus, it *would* be his fault if something happened to her. Hugo has beef with Julius, not Lucy. Whatever he did to Lucy, I'm sure it would be done to harm Julius.

After my harsh words, Julius just shook his head and headed to the bathroom for a shower. I was too upset to follow after him. Lucy and I just made up and now she was possibly gone forever. I couldn't believe I hadn't been talking to her because of a guy I didn't even care about. I was mad at myself for neglecting my best friend and taking it out on my husband.

I stripped down to my birthday suit and laid horizontally on the bed. I propped myself up with my elbows and waited for Julius to enter. After a couple minutes, he walked in with his towel around his waist.

"Come here," I said. He paused for a second and then finally walked over to me. He stood between my legs and I sat up. "I'm sorry for what I said. I would never forgive myself if something happened to Lucy. I just wanted to place the blame elsewhere," I said looking up into his eyes.

He smirked and pushed me back. He lifted my legs and then dropped his towel to the floor. His long thick dick was standing at attention already, and I was ready too. We only had sex once while being out here in Noblesville, and I missed our intimate connection. He slid into me and stroked me nice and slow.

"Ooohh fuck," he moaned. "I ain't been fucking you," he added.

"I kno- ahhh Juuuu," I purred as I wound my hips onto his dick.

"Damn, Nat. Keep doing that shit," he whispered as he watched his dick go in and out of me. As I wound my hips, he pumped me in a circular motion. "Ahh, uhhh, fuck babe," he groaned. I loved when I could get him to moan. He pushed my thighs towards me a little and threw his head back.

"Nah daddy, look at me when you cum," I said using his words.

He looked back down at me and smiled. He sped up his pumps, beating it up while staring me in the eyes.

"Uhh, Juu, ahhh," I cried out as he thrust into me. I looked up at him, and he was biting his lip with his sexy ass. That turned me on to the max and I released all on his dick.

"Ooohh fuck," he grunted as he exploded with me.

With his dick still inside me, I tugged on his wrist telling him to come closer. He lowered down onto me and wrapped my small body tightly within his strong arms. He dipped his tongue in my mouth, and we lay their kissing passionately for about twenty minutes straight.

"Rashad, you take a separate car," I said to my brother.

It was 9:58pm and we were getting ready to head out to Hugo's warehouse. I needed Rashad to take a separate car, so that once he got Lucy he could bounce. I didn't want her being a witness to anything we did. If the police asked her any questions, I wanted her *I don't know* response, to be the truth.

"Okay, cool," he replied and nodded.

Rashad got into his car and then Dash, Leese and I, piled into mine. Rashad followed us to the warehouse and once we arrived, we parked in a dark area. We all watched the warehouse quietly, as it neared 11:30pm. I prayed to God that Lucy was here and alive so that Hugo would show up. The closer it got to 11:30, the more nervous I became that he had in fact killed her. I knew my baby would be devastated.

"This nigga better come tonight," Dash commented.

"If Lucy is still alive, he will," I replied.

I nervously looked over at the clock and saw it was 11:38pm. *Damn, come on Hugo. Come on.* I chanted in my head. I could tell everyone was thinking the same thing, because the car was dead silent. My phone buzzed and I saw it was Rashad.

Rashad: ???

Me: I know, let's just wait a few more minutes.

I prayed in my head for Lucy to still be alive. I needed her to be alive. My baby girl would be distraught if her best friend was dead from getting caught up in my shit. I knew when she said she would never forgive me, she meant that shit. The clock now read 11:45pm and I was about to crank up the car and leave, until I saw Hugo's black truck pull up. I let out a sigh of relief and then put my game face on.

After a couple seconds, he exited the car and headed inside the warehouse. *Thank you God*, I thought. The four of us exited the car and surrounded the place in our assigned spots. I explained to Rashad that Hugo kept his hostages in the back by an escape door. He was to count to twenty-five from the time I walked in, and then come in the back door. By that time, I would have Hugo in another room. I walked through the warehouse towards the back hostage room and exhaled when I saw Lucy knocked out in a chair. Hugo was standing in front of her with his finger under her nose to check if she was breathing.

"What's up pimp?" I spoke. Hugo jumped and spun around on his heels to face me.

"Just the punk muthafucka I been looking for," he smiled and walked towards me.

Come on Rashad, I thought as I looked behind Hugo. Finally, Rashad slipped through the door and started to untie Lucy quietly.

"Why have you been looking for me?" I asked laughing.

"I should've gotten rid of your ungrateful ass years ago," he said as I watched Rashad carry an unconscious Lucy back out.

"You always been-"

POW!

POW!

I was cut off by the sound of two gunshots. I hoped it was Dash or Leese taking somebody out and not the other way around. Hugo caught wind of the festivities and reached for his gun. I couldn't pull mine fast enough, so I rushed him making him lose the grip on his. I quickly pulled mine and emptied five shots into his head.

As I was running out, I spotted Bianca sprawled out in another area. A pool of dried blood was coming from her head, and she was definitely dead. It was a bittersweet moment for me. I wanted to kill Bianca myself, but then again, I couldn't wrap my mind around how far to the left our relationship had gone. It seemed like just yesterday we were laid up together as boyfriend and girlfriend. Now almost three years later, she was dead in a pool of blood and an enemy of mine. The fact that she was killed by Hugo or one of his people had me confused, but I didn't care at this point. I shook my head and proceeded to the route.

"Come on!" I shouted when I saw Dash and Leese by the front entrance and still intact.

Once I got out, Leese dragged the two niggas they shot into the warehouse and then poured some gasoline all over the place as fast as possible. After he threw the match in, we ran to the car and got the fuck out of dodge.

"We fucking did that shit!" Dash said laughing.

"Thank God, now we can head back to Charleston," I said exhaling and getting on the freeway to Noblesville. "Text Rashad and ask him where he took Lucy," I said while driving.

"He said to the hospital right now, then after that to his condo," Leese replied.

"Aight," I nodded.

I was still low-key tripping out about how Hugo and I went from like father and son, to enemies. I never thought in a million years that I would've been pumping bullets into the very nigga that put me on. I hated that it had to end this way but clearly, there was only room for one of us here and it was me.

"Lucy is alive and well," I smiled and hugged Natalia from behind. She was putting Jackson in his onesie on the changing table.

"I love you Julius!" she beamed and hugged me tight.

"I'm sorry she got caught up in this babe," I said as I followed her to the living room area.

"I know, but let's not sulk. We need to celebrate," she said bringing some champagne from the kitchen.

"You only nineteen, ma, I shouldn't even let you drink," I smiled and pulled off my sweatshirt.

"Let me? I'm your wife. We're equals," she smirked.

"You the best fucking wife a nigga could have too," I replied in a low tone, as I pulled her close to me. "Why are you tensing up?" I quizzed.

"Because you still make me nervous," she blushed.

I took the bottle out of her hands and dipped my tongue into her mouth. I ran my fingers through her hair as we sucked each other's lips. As I was leading her to the couch to make love, she stopped me.

"What ma?" I frowned. My dick was rock fucking hard.

"I want to drink some champagne first," she giggled.

I playfully smacked my lips and then plopped down on the couch. For the rest of the night, we watched movies and downed the whole bottle of champagne.

LUCY

BACK IN SOUTH CAROLINA

The crew finally returned to Charleston and I was just getting over what happened to me. After Hugo raped me, he tied me to a chair and just left me there to starve. I was only there for two days, so the most that happened was I peed on myself. I held everything else in. Team no anal sex, kept it tight enough to do that. I thought I was gonna die there, but somehow Julius and his brother found me. In my eyes, it was nobody but God that got me out of there.

I had just gotten home from having dinner with Natalia, and I was so happy to have my best friend back. Especially now that she said she didn't really hang out with Paula anymore. I never really cared for Paula, as I'm sure you guys could tell. She thought she was better than every damn body and that was not cool. It's nothing wrong with feeling yourself but damn girl, be humble. I hated chicks like her that had something to say about everybody else, like she was perfect. She thought because she snagged Rashad that she was big shit, but home girl was far from it in my eyes.

KNOCK!

KNOCK!

"Who is it?" I frowned. I wasn't expecting anybody and Natalia had just texted me that she was home.

"Rashad."

"Hey Rashad," I said opening the door. "What's up?" I quizzed, cocking my head to the side. I was definitely confused to say the least.

"I just came to check on you," he smiled. "Can I come in?" he asked and I nodded.

When Rashad rescued me, he was really good to me. He took me to the hospital to get checked out and stayed there with me the whole time. At first, I thought he was just doing it because Julius told him to, but I realized he was just being nice. Paula crossed my mind at times because I knew she hated me. It made it weird that her man was looking after me. I wanted to rub it in her stuck up ass face, but I decided to leave the petty Lucy in the past.

"Would you like a drink or something?" I offered as he sat down on my couch.

"You have drinks in here? How old are you again?" he frowned and laughed.

"Freshly nineteen, nigga," I smiled and rolled my eyes playfully.

"Young ass, but yeah, I will take whatever you got," he smiled.

Rashad was sexy as hell. He was tall, dark skinned, muscular and always rocked a fresh fade and goatee. The old Lucy would've fucked him in Paula's bed, but I was a new woman now. However, if she fucked with me, I would return to my old ways one time just for her.

"Here you are," I said handing him a Smirnoff ice in the Raspberry flavor.

"Thanks beautiful," he replied.

"You know, it's kind of weird that you're so nice to me when your girlfriend hates me," I laughed.

"She hates everyone and every damn thing," he scoffed. "Plus, that ain't my girlfriend anymore. I'm trying to move on from that." He shook his head and took a swig of the Smirnoff.

"Uh, sorry, didn't mean to hit a nerve," I responded.

"Nah, you good ma," he said licking his lips, as he stared at my body.

I had on an off-the-shoulder crop top and sweat shorts. My toned flat stomach was showing and my belly button was pierced. My short bob was now grown out a little past my shoulders and bone straight.

"I never got to thank you for taking care of me," I said and sipped my Smirnoff. I was trying to divert his attention away from my physique.

"You're welcome," he said and scooted closer to me. "Let me take you out Lucy," he added as he stared into my eyes.

"What about Paula, Rashad?" I frowned in confusion.

"Man, that ain't even a factor," he jerked his neck back.

"It *is* a factor for me. I'm not gonna go out with you when you have a girlfriend. I'm not some rebound that you can use when your main chick is tripping," I spat and pointed my finger in his face. I was serious too; I was done with coming second or being a nigga's little secret.

"You too good to be a rebound," he replied and took my finger into his mouth. All I could think about was how those lips would feel against mine. "Now is that a yes or no?" he questioned, biting his full bottom lip.

"Prove to me that you're single," I smiled, enjoying his aggressiveness.

"How?" he smiled back.

"Let's post a picture on your Instagram," I snickered because I knew that was petty as fuck. I didn't care though. Being the old Lucy was fun sometimes.

"You're a fucking trip," he smirked and held his iPhone up so that we could take a picture together. He draped his arm around me and kissed my cheek while I poked my lips out. I made that face just for Paula's ass. "What should I caption it?" he chuckled.

On to better things, I replied and we laughed. Well I'll be damned, that nigga posted it too.

"What's your IG name? I wanna follow you," he inquired.

"You Love Lucy," I told him and ran my tongue over my top row of perfect teeth.

"I just may start to," he winked and I blushed.

Rashad stayed over my house all damn night and had the nerve to try and spend the night. I respectfully declined, because I didn't want to tempt myself. On top of that, Lumar had a doctor's appointment tomorrow, and I didn't feel like having to get Rashad out of my house in time to take my son. I did see Paula blowing his phone more than a couple times though, and it made me laugh to myself. He made sure to ignore every attempt she made to contact him though. If he kept this up, he and I may have something here.

NATALIA

2 WEEKS LATER

Things were back to normal around here and I was happy. For once in my life, Julius was on the straight and narrow. He wasn't in jail, cheating, hitting me, and no outside niggas were trying to break us up. I was enjoying the normal married life a lot. All I was focused on these days were my kids and trying out new cupcake recipes for my bakery.

Today, Lucy and I were going on a little shopping trip. I hadn't been shopping in forever, and I was definitely in need of some retail therapy. I wished Paula could come, but she had been on one ever since that conversation we had when I was back in Indiana. I tried apologizing to her, but she just ignored my texts. I was sad about it at first but then again, I started out with only Lucy and I had no problem ending up with only Lucy. Paula was too irritable for my taste and I had no interest in dealing with her when my life was finally peaches and cream.

"Ms. Lucy is here," Winnie said peeking into my bedroom, as I spread lotion onto my legs.

I wore a simple canary yellow dress that hugged my small yet shapely frame. I wore brown sandals, gold jewelry and my hair in a single braid down my back.

"Okay, thank you," I smiled at Winnie as I stood up and gave myself the once over.

"Should I make extra for dinner tonight?" Winnie asked before leaving my bedroom.

"Umm, yeah, why not," I replied and grabbed my purse to leave.

"Bye honey," she said and lightly rubbed my back as I walked past her.

I kissed Winnie on the cheek and then went downstairs. Winnie had become like my mother over the years. I loved her like one and she treated me more like a daughter than my own mom did. My kids didn't even know Dalia, my mother, so I'm sure they'd think Winnie was their grandmother anyway. Honestly, I preferred it that way. I'd tried calling my mom but she never answered. When she did answer, she only wanted money or she would rush me off the phone.

Lucy and I were gonna go to the Towne Centre in Mount Pleasant, because they had the most stores that we wanted to go to. I mainly wanted to get some new tube dresses, my favorite, and some new outfits for Jackson. He was almost two so it was more fun to dress him now. He was growing out of his old stuff anyway. My baby boy was gonna be tall just like his daddy.

"So I have to tell you something," Lucy smiled, as we sifted through the clothes in a store named Francesca's. How ironic.

"What?" I cheesed when I realized she was blushing.

"Rashad and I went out on a date," she grinned and paused to see my reaction.

"Lucy, that's Paula's boyfriend," I frowned.

I was a little upset because I thought she had changed. Although I would rather Rashad be with Lucy since she was my best friend, wrong was wrong.

"Not anymore Nat. I made sure of it before I even went out with him. Plus, we ain't do nothing. We went to dinner, watched a movie at his crib and then I went home," she shrugged.

"You like him?" I asked even though her demeanor said it all.

"Yeah, I do. It feels grown up though. Not like with Menzo, or even

Marlon. With them, I felt like it was so triflin' and juvenile," she wrinkled her nose. "I know what I'm trying to say, but it's not coming out right," she chuckled.

"No, I get it. It was the same with Ju until he started to mature. Rashad is older than Julius, so I'm sure it does feel grown up," I laughed. "Grandpa Rashad and Lucy," I joked and we cackled.

"He's only two years older. And twenty-four is not too old for us, we're nineteen," she smacked her lips and smiled.

"That would be tight if y'all had a baby together. Our kids would be cousins," I said placing a hand on my hip.

"Damn, I ain't even had sex with him yet and you're talking about kids," she smiled. "Lumar is enough for me right now," she nodded her head yes.

Rashad was a nice guy and I had never known him to be shady to anybody. He was good to Paula, but I was starting to wonder what happened to them. Rashad was so into her and hounded Julius and I for weeks to hook them up. Whatever it was, it must've been bad because he basically worshipped the ground she walked on.

"Are you worried about Paula?" I finally asked Lucy, as we headed to Gymboree.

"Hell no, never was and never will be," she frowned up as if I insulted her.

"Don't you wonder what happened between them?" I asked her and she shook her head no, making me laugh.

After we finished shopping, we went to Longhorn Steakhouse to have dinner. We talked for a little bit more and she showed me some of the texts that Rashad had been sending her. He was definitely not playing any games when it came to pursuing Lucy, and I just had to know what happened between him and Paula.

"**J**ulius," I said as he kissed down my stomach. We were lying in bed, preparing to make love.

"Yes babe?" he asked still kissing down my stomach.

"What happened between Paula and Rashad?" I inquired.

"I'm about to eat your pussy and you thinking about my brother and his ex?" He sounded like he was frowning. He went back to kissing and biting my inner thighs, almost making me forget my question.

"Julius."

"Yes, Natalia?" he exhaled in frustration.

"Can you please just tell me?" I quizzed.

"She was nagging or some shit like that," he appeared to shrug his shoulders. It was kind of dark so I couldn't really tell.

"He wants to break up with her over that one thing?" I turned my lip up.

Julius exhaled and brought his head up from between my legs. He positioned the head of his dick at my opening and thrust into me before I could even protest.

"Ahh, Juuu. Why did you-uhhh," I cried out in pain and pleasure. He usually went in inch by inch, but I guess he wanted to shut me up.

"I knew that would get you quiet," he whispered as he lowered himself closer to me. He dipped his tongue into my mouth and pumped me at a medium pace.

I was gonna find out what happened, one way or the other. However, it looks like tonight wasn't gone be the night.

ONE MONTH LATER

"Rashad!" Paula yelled standing over me.

"The fuck you yelling for?" I frowned sitting up.

I was so damn tired of Paula. The love I had for her had died months ago. When we first got together, I thought for sure we were gonna be married, but that changed after a couple years together. I told my brother she nagged me too much, but really it was because I found out she was grimy and sneaky.

She was trying to purposely get pregnant, thinking it was gonna make me marry her. She brought up marriage constantly and when she saw that I had no interest in doing it anytime soon, she tried to get pregnant. She had a weird obsession with being like Natalia. Everything that happened to Natalia, she wanted the same to occur in her life. Every decision she made was based off what Natalia did in the same situation. She already had a daughter, Gabby, so I didn't understand the rush to make a new baby.

The first sign that she was on some bullshit, was when I caught her running a sewing needle threw my condoms, while they were still in the wrapper. The holes were so small that if I didn't catch her doing it, I wouldn't have known it was tampered with. When I caught her, she acted like she was just drunk and didn't know what she was doing. I tried to let that go and decided just to have a fresh pack stashed somewhere safe. Then she tried to tell me she was on birth control and we didn't need condoms. When I asked to see the pills, she couldn't provide the proof. What kind of shit is that? Even if she had a baby, we would not be getting married. This was not the Paula I met a year ago.

At this point, I was no longer interested in being her boyfriend, friend, associate, nothing. I wasn't lying to Lucy when I told her Paula and I were no longer. I knew Lucy before Paula, but never paid attention to her. When I spent that time with her back in Indiana helping her get better, I realized how sexy and beautiful she was. Her personality was so refreshing, and it was a nice break from crazy ass Paula.

I usually preferred brown to dark-skinned girls, but I would make the exception for Lucy. Lucy had a smooth toasted vanilla complexion and a sexy ass body. Good Lord, my dick was getting hard just thinking about it. She also had a perfectly round ass, small waist, nice size titties and toned sexy legs. I loved when she wore crop tops and shorts because it was like pure artwork with legs.

"So you got a new bitch already?" she frowned down at me, pulling me from my fantasies about Lucy.

"Man, you and I are not in a relationship anymore ma. You're in no place to question me," I said standing to get ready to shower. I was kicking myself for not taking the key she had to my crib.

"So that's it? We been together for almost two years and now it's just over?" she yelled at my back.

"You tryna trap me ma! I ain't with that shit. Go be with a nigga that wanna get trapped," I shrugged. It'd be different if she just ended up pregnant but trying to trick me? That's some foul shit.

"Nah, I'ma be with you," she replied calmly and chuckled nervously. I'm telling y'all she was off her rocker.

"Okay," was all I said before going to the bathroom to shower.

I dressed and grabbed my phone and keys before heading out the door. As I walked through my living room, I saw Paula sitting on the couch bouncing her leg.

"Yo, you gotta go. I'm about to leave," I said frustrated.

I was over our arguments and debates we had all damn day. Paula showing up to my crib and yelling over me to wake me up, was routine for the past month. She would drop Gabby off at Kindergarten, then shoot over here to go off.

"Not until you sit and talk to me Shad," she replied folding her arms over her chest.

I threw my head back so far in irritation, you would've thought I was about to do a damn back bend. I sat down on the couch with her but much further away. I don't know why I was surprised; we did this shit every morning unless I spent the night with Lucy.

"Talk," I said dryly as I dropped my face in my hands.

"I wanna fix this babe. We've been together too damn long to just throw it away. I know I was wrong for trying to trick you into getting me pregnant, and I'm sorry. I love you so much Rashad, and I know you still love me," she pleaded trying to take my hand into hers. I snatched it away to run it over my face, and then paused to gather my thoughts.

I scooted closer to her and took her hands into mine before speaking. "Paula, I love you, but I'm not in love with you anymore. I haven't been happy for a while, and then you trying to trap me was just the icing on the cake. I've been feeling trapped with you and I don't want to feel like that anymore ma. I care about you, but I don't want this," I replied honestly. It felt good to finally say how I had been feeling for the last eight months. I never wanted to be that guy that chased a woman just to break her heart, so I'd held it in all this time.

"This is Lucy. Lucy has got you feeling this way," she scowled. "Don't let that streetwalker cloud your judgment babe," she pleaded with me. It was almost laughable, but I held in my laughter because I knew she was serious.

"I felt this way before Lucy, ma," I responded, shaking my head. "Way before Lucy, I'd become miserable."

"So what, are you guys dating?" she asked with furrowed eyebrows.

"Yeah, we're just seeing where it goes right now. I really don't want to discuss this with you and I have somewhere to be Paula," I said standing. I was really feeling Lucy and thinking about making it official; however, Paula didn't need to know that.

"You fucked her?" she glared at me.

"Unfortunately no," I exhaled heavily, because I couldn't wait to smash Lucy.

Paula stood up and stared at me, then quickly left my house. Thank God.

"That Goosebumps movie was so good," Lucy smiled as we walked into my house.

"I bet it was, eating all my damn snacks," I chuckled as I locked the door behind her.

"Sharing is caring," she cheesed, flashing her beautiful smile.

"Yes, but I tried to buy you your own and you said 'nah I'm good,'" I replied imitating her voice, and she laughed.

"Whatever nigga. That popcorn wasn't that good anyway," she smacked her lips.

"You weren't saying that when you were grabbing handfuls and stuffing it into that big ass mouth of yours," I joked.

"I'm sure you enjoyed watching me eat," she poked her lips out and I laughed.

I walked over to her and wrapped my arms around her small waist. She draped her arms over my shoulders, and lightly trailed her fingers up and down the nape of my neck. I leaned down, pressed my lips against hers, and started to suck her lips. I backed her into my bedroom as we continued to kiss hungrily. I was still smashing Paula, but I wanted to feel Lucy bad. We reached the bed and I pushed her onto it lightly.

"Rashad wait, I don't know about this," she said pulling from our kiss.

"Why?" I asked as I panted heavily.

"To be completely honest, I'm tired of giving my body up with no commitments. I've done it in the past, and it always left me heartbroken. I'm not asking that you be with me, but I'm just saying I can't do this …like this," she explained with a concerned expression.

"Well let's do it then," I said pecking her soft lips.

"Do what?" she quizzed looking into my eyes.

"Let's make this official," I said pulling her closer to me as I laid between her legs.

"Your real girl, like no funny stuff?" she questioned smiling.

"No funny stuff. Just me and you," I smiled.

She smiled back and pulled me close for a kiss. We undressed each other, trying our best not to break our kiss while doing so. I kissed all over her beautiful physique, and then went to devour her hard nipples as I fingered her.

"Uhh, Rash- ahhh," she cooed.

Once she exploded onto my fingers, I sucked off her juices and then dipped my head down to suck on her clit. I took my fingers and plunged them back inside her, as I continued to attack between her hips. I licked up all her juices once she exploded, and trailed my tongue back up to her mouth. I was about to do all kinds of shit to this sexy ass body of hers.

I placed her legs over my shoulders and slid deep inside her snug walls. It was so wet, warm, and tight, and I knew I may not last too long. I started off slow while sucking on her full lips. I felt as if I didn't have enough mouths and hands to do all that I wanted to do.

"Rashaaad, what are you doing to me," she whispered as I pumped in a circular motion.

After she came, I flipped her on all fours, and then proceeded to suck on her clit from the back until she exploded again. I bit her smooth, round, ass making her cry out in pleasure. I slid into her from behind, and spread her cheeks to watch my work.

"Shit," I moaned in a low tone.

"Shaadd, mmm, uhhh," she whimpered in her soft voice.

I sped up my strokes, watching her ass jiggle. She looked back at me and her sex faces turned me on to the max. I leaned down and pulled her bottom lip into my mouth, as I pumped away. I sucked her lips, and wrestled with her tongue until I exploded in her from behind.

I just exploded in her, fuck, I thought as I panted heavily.

The saying "life isn't fair" is all too true. How is it that I do everything right and hoe ass Lucy does everything wrong, yet she ends up with Rashad? The term "hoes is winning" is really true. The bitches that spread their legs for anybody always end up getting the best niggas, while the chicks with morals like myself, always end up alone and single.

I totally understand that what I did was wrong. I should've never sabotaged his condoms or made him think I was on birth control, but I wanted what the people around me had. I wanted marriage, the *new* baby, the house, everything. But no, Rashad wanted to continue being a little ass boy, continuing to shack up, fuck and play temporary daddy to my daughter, Gabby. Julius and Rashad had the same blood running through their veins, so why didn't they want the same fucking thing and at the same fucking time? I was a better woman than Natalia, so Rashad should've been trying to hurry up and lock me down. Shit, even Julius should've been looking this way.

I mean, I was a college graduate with a good life ahead of me. I lowered my standards to be with a damn dope boy, and this is how he does me? Rashad was beneath me, but I still gave him a chance because he was sexy. He should be begging to get a bitch like me pregnant. This is what happens when you date niggas that aren't on your level. I gave that nigga a chance and he didn't even appreciate it.

Now back to Ms. Lucy Ouistin. A nineteen-year-old single mom, with plenty bodies under her belt, and whose education stops at a high school diploma. It's laughable that he would shoot for something so low on the totem pole. Yeah, I was a single mom too, but you don't go from diamonds to rhinestones, and that's definitely what he was doing. Lucy wasn't even a cubic zirconia in my eyes. I chuckled at my thoughts.

I was gonna go talk to Natalia today and see if she wanted to help me break them up. She and Lucy weren't cool anymore, so I knew she would be down to get back at her. Plus, she and I were best friends now, so she had no choice but to comply. If she didn't, I would take her down too.

"Paula?" Natalia frowned when she opened the door.

"Hey boo!" I smiled as I walked in her house as if we'd been on good terms this whole time.

I followed her to the den area, so we could sit down and talk. The last time we had any communication, she insulted Rashad's and my relationship. I was gonna forgive her though, because I needed her help in getting rid of Lucy. After that though, I was gonna check her ass for downplaying me and *my* nigga.

"Would you guys like some passion fruit tea?" Winnie peaked in to ask us.

"Yeah, thank you Winnie," Natalia half smiled. "So Paula, I didn't even think we were still friends," she stared at me with a confused expression.

"I know, I forgive you though," I nodded.

"Forgive me for what?" she frowned.

"For insulting my relationship. For saying that Rashad and I weren't as serious as you and Julius," I turned my lip up. Was she dumb? *Calm down Paula*, I said to myself.

"I didn't insult you, Paula. I was trying to make you feel better by stating facts," she replied like the fool that she was.

"Whatever, I have plenty of facts on you and Julius, but I'm sure if I said them it'd feel like an insult," I fake smiled. She didn't want to go there with me.

"Like what?" she asked in a snobby tone. Was she crazy? All the shit I knew about their situation and here she was acting like we'd just met.

"Like the fact that he cheats on you all the time and that he hit you a lot," I said in a condescending tone. Maybe after I knocked her ass down a couple notches, she would snap out of her fantasy world.

"Correction, he *used* to cheat and *used* to hit me all the time," she fake smiled.

"Natalia, this is not what I came here for," I said defeated.

"Then what did you come here for?" she raised a brow. I wanted to slap her ass but that wouldn't help me.

"I need you to help me come up with something to get Rashad back. I need to get Lucy away from him," I replied.

"What?" she frowned. "I don't do stuff like that," she added in that innocent tone of hers.

"No one is gonna get hurt," I lied.

"Lucy will and maybe even Rashad," she said.

"Oh, and what about me? I'm just supposed to let her have him?" I bucked my eyes.

"Yes, let him go, and if it's meant, he will come back," she smiled.

"I don't believe in fairytales like you, Nat. Are you gonna help me or not?" I said standing up.

"Not," she responded.

"Cool, you remember this bitch," I said. I downed the tea Winnie brought us and then stormed out.

Operation *get rid of Lucy*, just became *operation get rid of Lucy and Natalia*.

I sat inside my Lexus, filing my nails. I was waiting for Lucy to come out of her cosmetology class. I was gonna give her a chance to bow out gracefully, before just taking the bitch out.

The clock read 3:00pm, so I prepared myself to get out the car. I knew she would be coming out in about ten minutes and I wanted to catch her as soon as she walked out the door. I jogged across the street and leaned up against the wall to wait for her.

"Lucy!" I called out as she walked outside.

"Yes?" she raised a brow as she turned to face me.

"Can I talk to you for a second?" I asked.

"You already are," she spat. *Don't hit her Paula. Don't hit her,* I chanted to myself.

"I'm not sure if you're aware, but Rashad is taken. We are actually about to have a baby," I smiled and rubbed my baby-less stomach.

"Oh word?" she laughed as if I'd just told the funniest joke.

"Word," I nodded.

"Well, you are right about one thing boo, Rashad *is* taken. He's *my* man for sure. Now as far as you being pregnant, I'm gonna go out on a limb here and say yo' ass is lying," she cocked her head to the left. "Didn't he leave because you *tried* to get pregnant, but by the grace of God, failed?" she smirked.

"Look bitch, I tried to be nice but you're making that real hard for me. Now either you stay away from Shad or pay for it with your life. Is he worth it?" I said through gritted teeth.

"Well, I usually would've said no, but seeing how bat shit crazy you've become, he must be worth it," she laughed. What was funny to her? I was serious! I was serious!

"Alright, well make sure to shoot me your mother's address so I can make sure to invite her to your funeral," I smiled and turned on my heels to leave.

There, you can't say I didn't give her a fair chance to live. I damn near begged her to save her own life, and she refused. Anything that happened to her at this point was all her fault.

JULIUS

Since our honeymoon, Natalia and I hadn't been on a nice trip. Since everything was going smoothly, I booked us a trip to Venice, Italy. This time, we were bringing Winnie, Harmony, and Jackson, because I wanted it to be a family trip as well. I also wanted Winnie to enjoy herself and get away. Rashad was bringing Lucy, and I knew that Paula was gonna have something to say about it. Natalia had already told me she came over yelling out threats and shit. I wasn't feeling that, but how harmful could she be, right? That was also for Rashad to deal with, not me.

We were staying at a hotel called Ai Cavalieri di Venezia, in Venice. We chose to stay in the royal suites, which were fit for kings and queens. All the curtains and bedding were white and gold and the bathrooms were all white marble, with hints of chestnut brown. The place was beautiful and I felt like royalty.

"I don't even know which one I like better," Natalia smiled as she toured our suite with Harmony in her arms.

"You mean between this and the one in Paris?" I smiled as I laid Jackson down.

"Yeah, this is so beautiful honey," she beamed.

"Here you go with that honey shit," I chuckled as she walked up to me.

"You don't like it?" she laughed.

"I *love* anything you do," I smiled down at her.

"Well, let me put her to sleep and then we can do some other things you love," she replied biting her sexy bottom lip.

"Sounds like a plan," I winked.

"I feel like a queen or something," Winnie joked as we sat down at the restaurant.

Ristorante Quadri was our restaurant of choice. Just like our room, it reminded me of a dining area for a king. It felt as if King Henry Tudor dined here before, just because it had that look. There were men playing violins and since it was nighttime, all the beautiful lights were on. The food was pricy, but it was supposedly the best place to eat here in Venice. This city was extremely romantic I was starting to see.

"I've been so hungry these days," Lucy commented as she looked over the menu and adjusted Lumar in her lap. Rashad looked worried when she said that and I wondered why.

Rashad was always careful in the bedroom like myself, so I knew she couldn't have been pregnant. I low key got Natalia pregnant on purpose, but was just in denial of my actions and feelings. I was immature and wasn't sure what the hell was wrong with me. It was hard for a nigga like me to admit I was in love back then.

After figuring out what half of this shit was, we went ahead and ordered our dishes. I was starved from traveling all day and couldn't wait to dig in. I kept seeing my brother carry a worried expression, and I knew something was up. I just hoped it wasn't too bad because I was getting used to living without any problems and enemies.

"You can share with daddy because mommy is hungry," Natalia joked as she handed Jackson to me. Harmony was sleeping in her carrier, in between Natalia and Winnie.

My wife was so perfect. She was beautiful, smart, sweet and most of all she loved a nigga. All the shit I did to her and she still loved me the same; maybe even more. Sometimes, I couldn't believe the way that I used to treat her. I couldn't imagine putting my hands on her and I hated to think about it. I was really crazy as hell back then.

Dinner was actually really good and I was relieved that we hadn't just wasted money on bullshit ass food. Rashad loosened up during dinner and was hella cozy with Lucy. I thought she was just a rebound at first, but I was seeing that he actually fucked with her. Afterwards, we toured around the city since we thankfully brought the strollers. A couple of hours went by, and we headed back to the room after realizing how late it was.

"I love you baby," I said once we walked into the bedroom of the suite.

"I love you too," she beamed.

I picked her up and she wrapped her legs around my waist. We sucked each other's lips slowly and gently, as we undressed one another. I laid on my back and she mounted my rock hard dick. She pushed herself down on it and we moaned in unison. She rocked her hips and bounced slowly, just the way I liked it. My mouth watered at the sight of her small perky breasts bouncing, and her stomach muscles slightly flexing. She placed her small hand on my abs for leverage, as she bit her lip.

"I'm cumming Ju," she cried out.

I gripped her small waist tightly and then rubbed my hands up and down her sweaty body. I reached around the back of her, then squeezed and smacked her small, round, fat ass.

"Fuck Nat. Ahhh, shit," I moaned in the way only she could make me do.

I pulled her down close to me, as she released on my pole. I pulled her soft lips into my mouth, and dipped my tongue into hers. I flipped her over so that now I was on top, with my dick still inside. We were sweating like crazy, and she looked so sexy to me. I licked her beautiful face, as I felt my nut rising.

"You're so fucking sexy to me baby girl," I whispered as I thrust into her hard but slow.

She whimpered softly and stared into my eyes the way I liked her to. I sucked her chin and then caressed the sides of her smooth, sweaty thighs. I pushed one of her legs back and went ham as I bit her inner thigh by the knee. You could hear the sound of how wet she was, our moans and our sweaty bodies pressing against each other. I wished I could record that shit to listen back.

"Ahhhh!" we yelled out in unison as we both exploded.

We hugged each other tightly, as our bodies jerked together. I couldn't get enough of her.

"Don't let me go Julius," she whispered as we kissed, still in one another's embrace.

It was the last day of our vacation. We had been here for one whole week and I was not ready to get on that plane tomorrow. I needed this to last forever. I saw why people moved out of America to places like this. It was so relaxing and just all around different. People seemed so much nicer and welcoming than in America.

Today we were gonna go on a tour in a gondola. Lucy didn't really like water, so she was scared to go. I always saw them on movies and couldn't believe that I was gonna be on one. I made sure my phone was on and charged, so I could take as many pictures as I needed to.

"Why aren't you dressed Ju?" I asked when I walked into the bedroom.

"Cause I'm tryna figure out why Marlon is calling and texting you," he said angrily as he sipped on some Hennessey.

"I-I don't-"

"Don't say you don't know," he cut in.

"But I don't," I replied confused.

"Well according to these texts, he misses and loves you so when we get back you can be with that nigga," he said tossing my phone on the bed.

"No, I'm gonna be with my husband. I don't know why he is

texting me Julius, stop acting like that," I frowned. I was so irritated. He knew damn well I had never and would never cheat on him. I wondered what made him so paranoid.

"How I know you ain't lying?" he asked twisting up his perfect caramel face.

"Never mind," I replied and grabbed my purse.

"Oh, so you don't give a fuck?" he raised a brow like he was surprised.

"I'm tired of you always accusing me Julius, especially when you're the only one who has cheated," I said feeling myself get sad.

"Yeah, as far as I know," he responded nastily.

"Okay, are you coming?" I inquired, ignoring his bratty attitude.

"Nah, I'm not. Fuck you," he spat.

"Okay, Winnie has the babies so you can go out if you want," I said and turned to leave.

Before I made it to the door, he grabbed me and carried back into the bedroom. He closed the door behind him, but didn't say anything.

"Julius, let me leave. I don't wanna be late for the tour," I frowned and walked to the door.

He blocked the doorknob and then took my purse off my shoulder. He backed me over to the bed, and then raised my dress.

"Stop Ju, I have to go," I whined.

He tugged my panties down, almost ripping them and then spread my legs. He dropped down and started to play with my clit while licking and sucking.

"Fuck," I moaned in a low tone.

He pushed my legs back and attacked me with his tongue and lips. I felt myself about to explode and ran my fingers through his soft fade. He looked up into my face, as I bit my lip hard. A tear slid down my face as he worked his magical mouth.

"Ahh, shit Ju," I yelled as I came hard. He licked between the slit, making me jump and jerk. He always made me cum hard as hell. My legs were trembling, so I had to sit there for a couple minutes.

"Yeah, sit that ass down and wait for me," he smiled as he went to the bathroom to get ready. I hated but loved his psycho ass.

Once Julius was ready, we left to go on the tour. We were late for the one we originally wanted to go on, so we had to wait for the next one. I usually would've been mad, but that orgasm he brought me to made me realize that being late was worth it.

We were finally able to get on, and I was extremely excited. It was such a romantic ride and I was glad that Julius suggested we ride separate from his brother and Lucy.

"I'm sorry about earlier," Julius said as he pulled me into his lap.

The gondola was still going and now it was dusk. The sun was setting, so the lights in the city were on, making it real romantic. I felt like I was in some beautiful dream or Disney fairytale. I was having such a good life, compared to when I first met Julius, that I feared someone would wake me up and say I was in a coma.

"It's okay," I replied.

"It's not okay. I don't need you falling out of love with me," he said moving my hair out of my face. He half smiled as if he was joking, but I knew he was serious.

"I could never do that," I frowned.

"You say that now," he smiled.

"And I'm gonna be saying the same thing seventy years from now too," I said caressing his handsome face.

I just wished Julius would realize that I'm never going anywhere. Anytime we broke up, it was because of him. I've always loved him and wanted him; it was always he who didn't know what he wanted. I should be the one scared he was gonna fall out of love. Hopefully now he saw that I was always down for the cause.

"Me too," he replied to my previous statement.

"Pinky promise," I smiled and held up my pinky.

He chuckled and wrapped his big pinky around my small one. I pecked his lips and he dipped his tongue in my mouth. We kissed heavily for the rest of the ride.

LUCY

3 WEEKS LATER...

I sat in the bathroom, on the floor and stared at the positive pregnancy tests in my hands. I'd taken five of them and they all came back the same. *Not again*, I thought. I knew all too well why Rashad left Paula and a baby had a lot to do with it. But it's not my fault he didn't use anything. The first time we got caught up in the moment, but most times after that, especially in Italy, he never even reached for one. I would suggest it, but he would never use one. I felt so dumb for not making him use it.

Although I knew Rashad and I would be over because of this, I couldn't kill my baby. I chose to let Rashad run up in me raw and I needed to take responsibility for it. But damn, I'm only nineteen and this would be my second baby. However, if Natalia could do it, so could I. I told myself that in order to feel better about the situation.

Rashad and I were now living together and I knew he would be home soon. I needed to tell him now so that I could get this over with. I wasn't trying to be three months in, and stressing over a break up. I wanted to do it now and then have a healthy pregnancy hopefully.

I decided to cook his favorite meal, in hopes that he would be in a better mood. He loved shrimp scampi and that was easy to cook, thank God. I cooked his food and set the table nicely. I dimmed the lights and lit two candles to make it more romantic. Why was I doing this knowing that this was gonna be everything but romantic? I don't know… a girl can hope though, right?

"What's all this babe?" Rashad chuckled as I led him into the dining room.

"I thought I would do something nice for you," I cheesed nervously and pulled his chair out.

"Mmmm, thank you," he kissed my lips and then sat down.

I went and retrieved his plate, then sat down with him to eat as well. I was starving and on edge, which was a bad combination. I gulped down my juice, as Rashad drank his wine. I was hoping he didn't inquire as to why I wasn't drinking the wine with him.

"You good babe?" he questioned as he stuffed the food into his mouth. His dark skin was so smooth, and I just wanted him to hold me in his strong arms once I told him the news. I knew it would be a much different outcome though.

"Rashad, I… umm… I'm having, well technically we-"

"What ma?" he frowned.

"I'm pregnant Rashad," I finally spit it out.

"Oh damn," he replied sitting his fork down.

"I know you don't want the baby, but I can't kill it," I added. He ran his hands over his face and exhaled heavily. "I'm gonna go back to my place, so you can have some time to digest this," I said standing up. It took every muscle in my body not to cry as I carried my empty plate to the sink.

"Hey," Rashad said in a low tone as he hugged me from behind.

"Hey," I replied drying off the clean plate.

"So we're having a baby?" he asked turning me to face him and I nodded. "That's not so bad right?" he smiled.

"I don't know," I shrugged.

"It's gone be alright, ma," he said kissing my lips. He pulled me closer to him and hugged me tightly.

"I thought you didn't want kids," I frowned.

"I didn't, but now that I have one coming, I'm realizing I do," he said looking down into my eyes. "Only because it's you though," he added as he lifted my chin.

I simpered and draped my arms over his shoulders, as he sucked on my lips. Thank God, my life seemed to be somewhat coming together.

"Babe, do you think Paula would actually try to do something to me?" I asked out of nowhere.

"Nah, why do you ask?" he frowned.

"She kind of threatened me a couple weeks ago," I shrugged as if it was nothing.

"What did she say?" he inquired frowning up even more.

"She asked me were you worth my life," I replied looking up into his brown eyes.

"Wow," he scoffed. "Nah, don't worry about her ma," he shook his head. I could tell something was on his mind, but I declined to question him about it.

"If you say so," I half smiled. I hoped he was right, because I was in no condition to fight off any crazy bitches.

Business seemed to keep on improving. I decided to keep the control I had over Indianapolis because shit, why not? I sent some of my trustworthy workers over there to make sure things ran smoothly and I flew out there twice a week on top of that. I knew it was greedy to keep control over two areas, but I didn't care. The more money I made, the better. I had so much money saved up and invested though, that I really didn't need another city.

I'd just gotten back from spending five days in Indianapolis, even though I was only supposed to spend two. I made sure to get some flowers and chocolates for my wife, because I knew she was gonna be upset. I'd told her I would only spend two days out of town whenever I went. I didn't want her thinking I was cheating, especially because I didn't have the greatest track record.

"Hey baby girl," I walked into the room with the flowers and candy.

Natalia was sitting on the bed with a box of pizza in her lap. She only had on a t-shirt and her long, thick, brown hair was hanging down. I loved seeing her dressed down like this, because she was so naturally beautiful. She looked at me and playfully rolled her eyes. I set the roses and assorted chocolates down and then sat on the bed next to her.

"Can I have a piece?" I asked.

"Nope," she smirked.

"Why not?" I fake pouted.

"Cause you've been gone too long. I have a new husband now," she smiled and bit her pizza.

"Where that nigga at?"

"He's in the bathroom, you'd better leave before he fucks you up," she cheesed and then burst into laughter.

"Well it's worth the risk," I said taking the pizza out of her hand and climbing on top of her to kiss her face. "He knows his wife got some good ass pussy, so he should understand," I joked.

"Ahh!" she laughed as I kissed all over her pretty face.

"I missed you," I said as I pecked her lips.

"I missed you more," she replied. "I'm still mad at you though," she caressed my face.

"Why baby girl?" I frowned.

"Because you were gone an extra three days," she pouted.

"But I talked to you the whole time," I smiled.

"I know, but there was something I wanted to tell you face to face," she said in a low tone.

"What?" I asked rubbing up her t-shirt.

"We're gonna have a new baby," she paused to see my reaction.

I kissed her soft lips, as my hands roamed her small body under her shirt. She draped her arms around my shoulders and sucked on my lips.

"You happy Natalia?" I questioned.

"Yeah," she responded slightly above a whisper. "Why do you ask?" she looked into my eyes intently.

"I just want to make sure that being married to me, having my babies and all this, is making you happy. I want to be sure you're not just doing this for me," I said.

"No, I love being your wife and a mommy," she beamed.

"I'm gonna get Clayton started on the construction of your cupcake shop too," I smiled.

"Really?" she asked as she searched my eyes with hers.

"Yeah, about time we made millions from them good ass cupcakes you make."

"I love you so much, Ju!" she squealed.

"I love you more, Mrs. Tate," I replied dipping my tongue in her mouth.

"The one and only," she added in between kisses.

"You know I was good the whole time I was gone right?" I raised a brow.

"Yeah, I know. Plus, I read all your text messages," she smiled and held up my iPad.

"How long have you been doing that?" I chuckled at her sneaky ass.

"Long enough," she laughed.

"Well, then now you know I've been faithful this whole time," I replied in a serious tone.

"I knew you were. I just check your texts to know what's going on in your businesses," she nodded.

"Yo' little nosey ass," I said tickling her. Natalia was ticklish as fuck and it made the shit funny as hell.

"I'm gonna peeee!" she yelled out laughing.

I chuckled and stopped tickling her to kiss her lips. I rubbed my hands back up her shirt to play with her nipples, as she massaged my hardening dick through my sweats.

I'd just met with Clayton and Julius about building up *Harmony's Bake Shoppe* and I was so excited. I wanted to name it after my daughter since we already had the winery named after Jackson. I couldn't believe that I was gonna own my own bakery. I loved to bake cupcakes and now I would be making my own money doing it. Julius wanted it in only my name, and I was happy to hear that.

I was on my way to Lucy's so that I could share the news with her. Ever since she's known me, I've always taken an interest in baking, especially cupcakes. I never thought I'd see this day and here it was. I smiled at the thought. I wanted to call my mother and tell her, but I knew she wouldn't even care. I needed to stop trying to build something with her that she didn't even want.

As I was making a right, a car drove around me onto the sidewalk and scraped my BMW truck. *What the hell?* I thought. They kept going, so I sped up while trying to take a picture of their license plate. After getting a couple snaps, I sped onto the side of them to try and get their attention. The windows were tinted and I saw they had no plans of pulling over. *At least I got the plate number,* I thought. I drove a little bit of ways past them and then I heard a gunshot. My back right tire busted and I swerved a little bit.

POW!

POW!

Two more shots rang out and my front right tire busted as well. I flew into the intersection as I tried to bring the car to a halt. I was screaming at the top of my lungs as my truck spun wildly in a circle. The car finally flew onto the sidewalk, where a light pole stopped it.

"Oh my God!" I screamed and then looked into the backseat to check on Jackson and Harmony. Thank God they were both sound asleep.

I let out a sigh of relief and then pulled out my cell phone to call AAA. My hands were trembling like crazy, making it harder to dial. I frantically looked around to see if I could spot the black Toyota Corolla that just tried to kill me. Once AAA informed me that they were on the way, I called my husband.

"Hell-"

"Julius, somebody tried to kill me!" I cried into the phone.

"What? Where are you?" he asked.

"I'm waiting on AAA, someone shot my tires while I was driving," I replied.

The Auto Club arrived about ten minutes later, around the same time Julius did. We removed Jackson and Harmony from my car and let AAA tow it to the shop. Julius drove the three of us home, while my car was being worked on.

"You said they shot at you?" Julius asked once we got home.

"Yeah, at first they just sideswiped me, so I took pictures of their license plate. I tried to get their attention, but the windows were tinted and they wouldn't slow down. Once I went on about my way, they shot my tires," I sniffled.

"Calm down Nat," he said holding me in his arms.

"I thought I was gonna die," I sobbed.

"Thank God you didn't," he replied in a low tone.

"Who would do this?" I asked.

"I don't know baby girl, but we're gonna find out. Send me the picture you took of the plate." One million thoughts appeared to be running through his mind.

"Okay," I said.

I was scared out of my mind that someone tried to kill me. Who could this be? It probably was another one of Julius' enemies. I hoped he got out of this game soon because first it was Lucy and now they were coming for me. They didn't succeed this time, but who knows when they would be back.

PAULA

The saying "misery loves company" is all too true. Since I couldn't be happy, no one could be happy around this mutha-fucka. I'm not the bitch you can go around fucking over. You don't cheat on Paula. You don't disregard Paula's feelings. You don't play Paula either. That's what everyone did and everyone was gonna pay.

Yep, I shot out Natalia's tires. I didn't give a fuck if her kids were in the car either. If she didn't want to join me, she would have to go down too. I don't play around when it comes to my man. They would've known that if they had ever looked into what happened to my daughter's father. Anyway, now that I had Natalia shaken up, it was time to go after the real culprit, Lucy.

I found out this hoe was pregnant by *my* fucking man! This just infuriated me even more. Was he really about to have a baby with a bitch he'd only been with for a couple months? He constantly reminded me that he didn't want kids of his own, and even broke up with me when I tried to get pregnant anyway. See what I mean when I say hoes stay winning? A bitch that's about something, like me, gets tossed to the curb when she tries to get pregnant. However, a hoe gets embraced when she gets pregnant by that *exact* same nigga.

"Julius will be gone around 11am," I told Marlon.

Marlon was still obsessing over Natalia and I was gonna help him get her. Since I couldn't kill her, why not have Marlon harm her. Marlon had clearly lost his marbles and I knew if he got near Natalia, he might hurt her. I was gonna help him break in her home so he could have his way with her ass. In my eyes, I was doing her a favor more than harming her. Marlon was a far better choice for Natalia. To my knowledge, he had never cheated or hit her ass, so she would actually be thanking me after this. I needed all the help I could get with these stupid hoes anyway.

"So we can't go tonight?" he frowned with his thirsty ass.

"No, give it a couple weeks Marlon. Julius is gonna be watching her like a hawk right now," I shook my head and he nodded.

***

I sat outside of Rashad's place, waiting for him to leave for the day. I knew his house like the back of my hand, since I'd lived with his ass for a year. He was gonna come home to a nice surprise once I was done. Once Lucy was out of the picture, I was sure he would come back to me. I was so anxious to get this over with, so Rashad and I could return to our normal life.

I sat up straight as I watched Rashad walk out, and leave in his car. I pulled my gun from the glove compartment and made sure it was loaded. I walked as if I was a regular person that wasn't about to commit a murder. I ran around back and busted the window to the bathroom. I climbed through the window and jumped down into the tub. I slowly walked out the bathroom and through the house. I listened intently to see where Lucy was. I finally heard her ratchet ass listening to Rich Homie Quan in the bedroom, so I made my way over. She was dancing in the bedroom that I used to share with my love. No worries though, I would be back in here soon enough.

"Sup bitch," I smiled as I walked into the room. She turned to me and saw I had the gun pointed at her.

"Paula, wait. What are you doing?" she frowned.

"I'm here to kill you bitch," I said as if she asked a dumb question.

"Didn't I warn you? I think I did. What did you tell me? You said Rashad was worth you losing your life, right?" I snickered as I walked closer to her.

"Over Rashad?" she twisted up her mouth. "Really Paula? This is ridiculous." Was she dumb? Who the fuck else was it over? I gave this stupid bitch a chance.

"Yes hoe! Over *my* man! You couldn't have Julius, so you thought you could slide in on mine? I don't think so boo," I said cocking the gun.

"Okay, just give me a chance to-"

Suddenly, I heard the front door open and I panicked. I quickly shot anywhere and once I saw blood, I ran back out the way that I came. I got back into my car and after about ten minutes, the ambulance pulled up. I was slightly upset that Lucy wasn't in a body bag. My heart broke as I watched Rashad sob while getting in the back of the ambulance with Lucy.

She lived, damnit. I could only hope and pray that she somehow suffered complications from her wounds. If she didn't naturally suffer, I would have to pay her a visit in the hospital. Lucy would not walk out of that hospital alive if it was up to me. After the ambulance left, I finally pulled off as well, somewhat happy with my accomplishment.

"Baby girl! We have to get to the hospital!" Julius barged into the house.

"Why, what's wrong?" I asked taking the bottle out of Harmony's mouth.

"Somebody shot Lucy ma," he panted.

"Oh my gosh!" I yelped.

Winnie took Harmony from me so that I could leave and see her. Julius and I sped down to Roper Hospital and I was so anxious the whole time. *Please don't be dead,* I thought. *Who was shooting at us? Why us?* I wondered. We pulled up to the hospital and I was getting out before Julius even parked well.

"I'm here for Lucy Ouistin!" I said to the nurse.

"Please wait over there with the other young man," the nurse replied dryly. I rolled my eyes and made my way over to Rashad, who had Lumar in his lap.

"Have they said anything?" I asked as I sat down next to him.

"They haven't said shit. She went into emergency surgery and I'm still waiting," Rashad replied. "I just want to know who would do this," he shook his head.

"I don't know bro, but I bet it's the same person that shot at Natalia," Julius replied. That comment put me even more on edge.

We all sat there, and no words were spoken, except by baby Lumar. Julius held my hand tightly and kissed the back of it, once he felt it was sweating. Finally, after an hour, a doctor emerged from the back. The three of us stared him down, hoping he was bringing news about Lucy.

"Lucy Ouistin's family," he said looking up from his clipboard. We all rose up and walked up to him without saying anything. "Who are you guys to the patient?" he asked.

"I'm her husband, and this is our son," Rashad spoke up and lifted Lumar a little. I half smiled at his response.

"The surgery was successful for Lucy, but she is in a coma at the moment," he exhaled.

I couldn't help but break down and cry. Julius hugged me tightly, as I sobbed hysterically into his chest. I silently prayed that God spared Lucy's life. I didn't know what I would do if she died.

"Can we see her?" Rashad asked slightly sniffling.

"Yes, you guys can. Only for an hour however," the doctor nodded.

"Thank you," Julius replied as we all followed the doctor back to Lucy's room.

"Y̲ou want Winnie to bring your dinner up?" Julius asked me as I sat in bed staring at the wall.

"No," I responded barely above a whisper.

"Baby, you need to eat, you're pregnant," he pleaded.

"What did she make?" I quizzed still refusing to break my stare from the wall.

"Fried chicken. You know you love her chicken," he half smiled. I didn't respond, as a tear spilled out of my eye. "I'm gonna bring you the food, okay?" he assured.

He stared at me for a couple seconds, then left to get my plate. A couple minutes passed and he re-entered the room with a plate of chicken, squash and mashed potatoes. He sat on the edge of the by me and then placed the plate into my lap.

"Here Nat," he said.

I picked up the fork and started to play around with the mashed potatoes, before finally tasting them. They were nice and hot, and I was starved. I continued to eat my food as Julius changed into his boxers only.

"Lucy is gonna be fine baby," he said after a couple minutes of silence.

"I hope so," I replied in a low tone.

"And I'm gone find whoever is coming for y'all," he said standing next to the bed. His abs turned me on, but I couldn't have sex while Lucy was in the hospital.

Julius walked to his side of the bed and then laid next to me. He turned on the TV and I looked over at him, as he yelled at the football game he had on. His frown made him look so sexy and I wanted to feel him so bad. Would it be bad for me to have sex with him? I hadn't let him touch me all week because of Lucy.

I finished my dinner and then got out of the bed. Julius glanced at me but then back to the TV. I wanted to have sex but I wouldn't feel as bad if *he* initiated it. I removed the t-shirt I had on, leaving me naked except for the thong I had on. I pretended to be looking for something and I saw Julius staring at me. I walked over to the bed and pulled the covers back as if I was looking in the bed for something. I climbed into the bed and got close to his sexy face.

"Can you get up really quick?" I asked.

He didn't say anything and just took my hard nipple into his mouth. He pulled my panties off, as his mouth stayed latched onto my nipple. He pushed me onto my back and climbed between my legs. My pussy was drenched, as I anticipated him entering me. He dropped down on top of me and poked at my opening. Like usual when we went without sex for more than three days, he had a hard time sliding in. He pushed my legs back and then slowly eased himself inside me.

"Ahhh," I whispered.

"You did that shit on purpose," he grunted as he stroked me. "Daddy has been missing this pussy though," he added and bit his lip while watching himself glide in and out of me.

I simply smiled as I ran my hand down his sexy flexing abs.

JULIUS

2 WEEKS LATER

Tonight I was having a little get together, to celebrate all that I've accomplished. I was still rocking with Indianapolis as I told y'all before, but now I had taken over Orangeburg, South Carolina too. I was now getting double shipments from Antonio and Bart and thankfully, they were able to fulfill them. On top of that, Club Rissani and Jackson Beach Winery were flourishing, making all the money I had look clean. No longer did I have to worry about the police questioning why a twenty-two-year-old had a BMW, Ferrari, Porsche and a mansion.

"I just want to toast to my team, my family and most importantly, my beautiful wife Natalia Tate," I smiled down at her and pecked her lips.

Everyone clapped and then continued to mingle and socialize. Natalia was trying to be sociable, but I could tell that all she could think about was Lucy. My brother Rashad stopped by for a little bit, but then returned to sit with Lucy at the hospital. He was worried about his baby that she was carrying, and I couldn't blame him. I was just thankful that he even stopped by to show his face.

"How are you feeling?" I asked, pulling Natalia to the side.

"I don't know. But don't mind me, I'm okay," she smiled. "Go mingle," she chuckled and waved around the party.

"Is this Mrs. Tate?" Bart walked up with his daughters not far behind him.

"I am," Natalia smiled with her pretty ass.

"Wow Julius. Nice," Bart nodded and smiled. "Mrs. Tate, these are my daughters Skylar and Leah," Bart added.

"Nice to meet you ladies, I'm Natalia," baby girl smiled.

"Natalia, nice," Skylar fake smiled. She's had a thing for me ever since I met her back in Los Angeles.

"She *is* beautiful Julius," Leah smiled and hugged Natalia.

"Thank you," Natalia nodded. "Okay babe, I'm gonna sit down before this baby starts to act up." She looked up at me and I kissed her lips.

"New baby on the way?" Skylar smirked when Natalia, Leah and her father walked away.

"That's right," I nodded.

"So you guys are still in love then, I see. I remember when she wasn't your wife," she smiled. Skylar was a pretty girl. She was brown skinned, long dark hair, nice shapely body and perfect teeth.

"That was years ago," I chuckled uncomfortably. Skylar was bad and only bad things would come along with me fucking her. Bad things like losing my family and my connect. She was not worth any of that and once I reminded myself of such, it was easy to deny her advances.

"Why don't you take my number Julius? Just in case things get sour," she licked her lips. "Shit, even if they don't get sour," she shrugged one shoulder.

"Are you a marriage counselor?" I asked playing dumb.

"If that's what you want to call it," she smirked. "You're worried about disappointing my father when you should only be worried about me," she added.

"No, I'm just a married man and I only want my wife. That's why I married her," I frowned.

"No man only wants one woman," she replied matter-of-factly.

"What makes you so sure?" I asked.

"Cause I have yet to see any man stay faithful. My own father has cheated on my mother here and there. If he can't do it, I'm sure a twenty-two-year-old man cannot," she responded.

"Well you're wrong, and that's all I'm gonna say to that," I said looking around the room.

I didn't need Natalia getting suspicious of Skylar and I. Unlike most niggas, I was actually scared of losing my wife. Natalia was my happiness and without her, you can only imagine what I would be like.

"I think you and I were always meant to be something Julius Tate," she added.

"Something like?" I raised a brow.

"Maybe I will end up being your second wife," she chuckled.

"Enjoy the party ma," I half smiled and walked away.

There were always bitches trying to tempt you. I swear, ever since women found out I was married with kids, they seemed to want me more. The amount of chicks multiplied, it appeared. I hadn't cheated on my wife in forever, and I planned for it to stay that way. Natalia deserved the best and she would have nothing less fucking with me.

NATALIA

Morning sickness was a bitch. I loved all my babies, but the beginning process was always so draining. Eating all this food, just to throw it up and eat some more. I did enjoy being able to eat whatever I wanted, and being able to send Julius out to obtain my crazy cravings. However, I just wanted to fast forward life, to the part where I could keep my food down.

Since I was sick, Winnie decided to take the kids out for a walk at the park. She said she needed the exercise and I needed the break. I was just gonna relax in bed, eat, watch movies and pray for Lucy. I had been visiting her every day, but I was too ill to do so today.

BOOM!

I heard the back door open and close, so I assumed Winnie was back. She had just left about fifteen minutes ago, so it was odd that she was back already. I hoped she wasn't though, because I knew my son was gonna be all over me. He was so attached to me. Usually I loved it, but I wasn't in the mood right now.

"Winnie?" I called out. "Winnie?" I called again when I got no answer.

I climbed out of the bed and then headed down the stairs slowly. I grabbed a knife from the kitchen and walked towards the back door. I was so scared that the person who had shot me, had come back to finish the job. I was sure that I was gonna die if they did return.

"I missed you baby."

I turned around to see Marlon standing there with a smile on his crazy face. His hair was a mess and his beard was so long, that he reminded me of a black Santa Claus. He was panting heavily and only had on jeans and a white t-shirt. First it was crazy ass Frank, and now psycho ass Marlon. I could only imagine how they would've acted, had we had sex.

"Marlon, why are you in my house?" I inquired. *How did he get past the alarm system?* I wondered.

"Someone close to you gave me the code. Don't worry about that though," he grinned as he started to walk towards me.

"What do you want?" I asked clenching the knife in my hands tightly.

"I want you, but I know you're married, so I just came to get what I'm owed," he replied licking his dry lips.

"What you're owed?"

"Yeah ma, you owe me some pussy. You strung me along, making me think I'd get some, and you never fulfilled that promise," he stared at me seriously. "I want it! I deserve it!" he boomed.

"Marlon, that was a long time ago. Plus, you slept with my best friend!" I said backing away as he came even closer.

"That is your fault! You pushed me away!" he yelled so loud that his voice echoed throughout the mansion.

"Marlon, I don't want to have sex with you," I cried.

"Well then I will have to take it," he smirked.

"You want to rape me? I deserve that?" I asked trying to stall. I hoped I could think of a plan or that Winnie would come home.

"I'm gonna have to rape you unless you lie down and let me," he folded his arms and pursed his lips. "It's the least you could do since you fucked over my brother," he added.

"Your brother?" I squinted my eyes in confusion.

"Frank, you little hoe," he spat and balled up his fists, as he slowly started to come towards me.

No wonder Marlon had an Indianapolis number when I first met him. What are the odds that I would start dating Frank's brother? That would explain why they both turned psycho.

I was scared as hell, so I ran to the phone to call 911. Marlon pounced on me and pinned me to the couch, making me drop the knife. I kneed him in the nuts and he fell back off me and onto the floor. I reached for the phone again, but he grabbed me from behind and pulled me away. He flipped me onto my back and got in between my legs. I dug my nails into his neck and scraped off as much skin as I could. I wanted to rip a damn hole into his neck. Whatever I needed to do to stop him from raping me, I was gonna do it.

"Arrggghhh! You fucking bitch!" he yelled letting me go.

He stared at me as he panted heavily, while holding onto his neck. I tried to dial but he charged towards me again at full speed. I grabbed the small Keurig machine off the table and bashed him over the head. He wobbled back a bit, but tried to keep coming, so I bashed him again. I kept banging him over the head until he finally hit the floor. Blood poured from his head, as he stared at the ceiling with his eyes bucked. *Did I kill him? Oh shit!* I thought.

"Marlon, get up!" I shouted slapping his face.

I felt his pulse, and got nothing. *Natalia, you just murdered somebody,* I said to myself. I looked around the living room and blood was every-where. *Call Julius!* I told myself.

"Natalia! What did you do?"

I snapped my neck to look at the person behind me, and my eyes almost popped out of my head.

BECOME A VIP READER!

*To join my mailing list text **SHVONNE** to **66866** and stay up to date! Also, join **Shvonne Latrice Reading Group** on Facebook!*